THE KELLY MAN

Nothing much happened in Grande Flat, in the remote longhorn country of Southwest Texas. But in 1878 the Kelly boy unexpectedly returned to town, and he was now a man of twenty-six. After that, the monotonous existence of the town returned to normal. Or almost.

Kelly had ridden quietly into the town he'd left as a boy. The townsfolk saw the long scar on his face, the gun strapped to his thigh. But they couldn't see what was inside him, the anger that brought him back after all these years to find a man he had to kill.

THE KELLY MAN

Will C. Brown

First published 1964 by Dell Publishing Co, Inc

This hardback edition 1997
by Chivers Press
by arrangement with
Golden West Literary Agency

ISBN 0 7451 4707 0

British Library Cataloguing in Publication Data available

Printed and bound in Great Britain by
Redwood Books, Trowbridge, Wiltshire

THE KELLY MAN

1.

Nothing much ever happened in Grande Flat, except for that one week in May, 1878, when the Kelly boy came back to town, and nothing much ever happened in the years thereafter. The village was one of those arrested Texas townsite mistakes, languishing in the creviced brush land beside the Del Rio–El Paso supply road. Grande Flat and its scattered look-alikes might have been someone's fond hopes once when the lumber was freighted west from San Antonio, but most of them were destined to droop stunted forever like a mesquite transplanted without enough tap root. The four winds came in their seasonal turn to buffet the settlement with fry and freeze and the red-grit dusts of spring. In time, the town looked as pointless in existence as the land about it and the people grew to look like the town.

Monotony was the name for Grande Flat and others of its frontier ilk in the remote longhorn country of Southwest Texas. Each of them was bleak evidence that Texans had fanned out too fast and with more high hopes than good sense, a cheerful trait of the times, after the doldrums of the Civil War and the diminishing of the Comanche dangers. The adventurous had cracked their bullwhips in crazy directions and talked big of booms, but there never was a boom at Grande Flat. Fate did not even do the village the dignity of giving it the county seat when the county was organized;

Kiowa City, a newer try, got it, thirty miles and a day's ride south.

Grande Flat built up a little after the war, when the new railroads in Kansas created a market for Texas trail herds.

One of the establishments and a landmark was Uncle John Hinga's combination stage stop, horse pens, and feed supply. There was the big general store owned by never-smiling Otto Wendel and one smaller competing store; the saloon managed by Ren Blankenship, who, at twenty-seven, had never married but sufficed with a series of Mexican women; a wagonyard, blacksmith, barber shop, stock pens, a sheepshearing shed, vacant lots of sickly broomweeds, and the scattering of houses with their stubby steel windmills hustling day and night in the backyards. There was a frame box school with rag-stuffed broken windows for the white kids and, some years later, the condescending gesture of an adobe room a hundred yards removed from it for the handful of Mexican pupils.

Everywhere beyond were the scattered cattle outfits that helped to keep the town alive; the mesquite flats broken by stands of tenacious cedars and prickly pear, red sandstone canyons, and beyond that just the brassy haze of infinity. Not many came to settle there later; still, not many left. If asked why they stayed in the harsh middle of nowhere, the populace likely would have had to think hard for a reason, and then probably nothing would occur to them except the simple logic that they stayed because they were already there.

Yet, beneath its surface dullness, Grande Flat was people; the hard-jawed Anglos, the Mexican shack dwellers; old people who had fought the Comanches, the middle-aged, the young. Out of sight inside them the whites secreted the common human juices of hopes, hurts, emotions, and devious unspoken things. Nobody knew what the browns thought for they were there on tolerence as the cheap muscle to do the hard or menial chores.

So Grande Flat, which was the name for monotony, had its internal blisters come to a head all at once in a rare unstripping of secrets and troubles; it had its bloodletting that week in May, when the Kelly boy rode back as a man of twenty-six as unexpectedly as he had departed six years before. After that, at least partially cleansed, with most of its festers opened, the town settled back to just what it always was to be. Or almost so. A few did not live to see the subsiding, and some later recalled the events from merely their individual perspectives of where they had happened to be standing at the time; for the rest there was not much change at all from their various human averages of wickedness and virtue.

The first one to see him was Mrs. Henrietta Forbes, who was working her bed of zinnia seedlings at the front of her house, the farthest one south before the road bent to loose itself in the greasewood roughs. From the corner of her eye she caught sight of a solitary rider emerging out of the stained-glass light of the sun-filtering road dust of early afternoon. Absorbed in her weeding, she gave this no thought until she sensed that he had slowed behind her. Then she half-turned on her haunches, as if some belated apprehension had transmitted itself. No expert on quick sizing-up of details, she nevertheless stared as if the rider somehow was due more notice than the ordinary passerby.

She saw the dust and stain on man, horse, and leather, but the man sat his saddle as if untired and alert. His eyes seemingly cut to her, yet were not quite visible beneath the shadowing brim of his hat. The middle-aged Mrs. Forbes felt flustered. She vaguely noticed the saddlebags, the carbine stock, the man's dusty black boots and whipcords, his gun belt and revolver butt. Mrs. Forbes, conscious of her tacky posture, was caught in uncertainty as to whether she was being improperly eyed by a stranger or this was some range rider off the cattle land she slightly knew and couldn't place.

The hoofs of the horse had changed for a few trot beats, indicating that the rider knowingly had slowed, then the tempo was resumed. The man touched his hat. His head briefly turned toward her, then away.

She plainly heard him say, "Good afternoon, Mrs. Forbes."

She jerked her chin in dumb reply. Then she was looking at his straight back where the sweat of travel had ironed his shirt flat across his muscles. Still caught in a squat at her zinnia bed, she twisted the other way, but it was too late to see the scar again. She only knew that the man's dark face had shown a thin white streak on its far side, a scar line from his temple nearly down to the tip of his chin. In the sunshine, his shadowed eyes had looked white and so had the long scar, in contrast to all else about him, which was darkly weathered.

Although he was just a passing rider, Mrs. Forbes resumed her attack on the baked caliche earth in some frustration and confusion. She could not think who the man was, although he knew her. It took some minutes of concentration with the zinnia working before a face and a time and a memory from six years back came together. She paused and glanced north toward the road where the rider was now passing the blacksmith shop. His head still was set straight but she felt that his eyes worked to each side from under his hat shadow.

"Well, I'll be!" Mrs. Forbes said aloud. "That man—that was the Kelly boy!"

The zinnias won't grow.

They never had. It was the alkali water. But he was pleased to have recognized Mrs. Forbes, glad to see her still trying. Then he fixed his attention for whatever else would be next in his nostalgic recognition. The blacksmith shop on his left, the frame fronts and adobes scattered down the street ahead, were as familiar as yesterday. It was the quiet 2 P.M. time, and the unchanged street scene was drowsy. A Mexican, squatted beneath a tree at the wagonyard, raised his head, dutifully touched his sombrero brim, and disappeared again under it.

He saw no familiar face anywhere and rode on to the far

10

corner of the second block and around to the pen at the back of Uncle John Hinga's adobe stage building.

The place was still and silent in the early afternoon sunshine. For a moment he remained in the saddle, taking in each detail of the back alley and the pens and stalls beyond. Then, as if something special saved, he shifted his glance to the adobe shack built on to the back corner of the main building. The plank door stood half-ajar and the top hinge was still bent, so the door sagged and he knew it lacked five inches of closing at night. The shed's doorway opened into the horse lot, giving direct access of mornings to the feeding chores without having to go through the kitchen in the rear of Uncle John's living quarters.

Saul Kelly dismounted and extended his hand through the gate slats to slip the chain fastener from its bolt and knew that he could have done it with his eyes shut. Nobody came while he was unsaddling and watering.

He started for the gate and the scene in the dusty sun rays stayed lifeless. On impulse, he changed his direction and entered the shed room. The iron cot was in the same corner, its covers unmade. The pieces of makeshift furniture looked the same. The floor had splinters and was bare except for a bug-eaten coyote pelt. In one corner a crude partition made a doorless closet. He glanced in there, seeing nothing but a jumble of clothes and assorted junk on the floor.

He turned quickly at a sound, and a gangling boy in overalls appeared outside the doorway. Kelly nodded, and the boy spoke in a voice that wavered on the changing tones of youth: "You want somethin' in here?"

The man relaxed from the first tautness of his turn. "This your room?"

"It sure as heck is. You want somethin'?"

"You work for Mr. Hinga? You the pen boy?"

"Yeah." The boy's interest had fastened to the man's thin white jawline scar.

Saul Kelly moved toward the door. "Nobody ever fixed that hinge, did they?"

The boy involuntarily glanced at the sagging door.

Saul Kelly murmured, "In the closet, there. Used to be a box of books. I don't see the books anywhere."

The boy considered, then said, "Never seen any. What kind of books?"

Kelly said thoughtfully, "Books about the world. All kinds. Somebody stored them here once. They would have told you about people and things far off, out where the winds blow from long before they get to Grande Flat. Too bad you didn't inherit them. They might have made the time pass here."

"Heck, what good are books?"

Kelly looked about the room. "They could egg you to spring this trap and see what's beyond. But never mind."

The boy gave ground as Kelly emerged. "Did you live here once, in this room?"

"Sure did. Six years. Same job as the one you're doing, I expect."

"Then you're—I heard your name. Saul Kelly?"

"That's right. John Hinga's my uncle. He about?"

The boy motioned toward the main building. Now his interest had shifted to the heavy butt of the Colt in Kelly's black holster.

Kelly gestured a so-long and strode to the gate, then around the pen to the kitchen door. A Mexican woman— not Maria Mendoza, the one he had expected to see— turned inquiringly from the cook counter as the tall stranger quietly crossed the room. In Spanish he spoke and said he was looking for Hinga. He walked on to the long hall- way and to the front room that served as a parlor, stage waiting room, and office.

John Hinga sat half-dozing in his old leather-bottomed chair with his sock feet propped on another chair. He came up from the last stages of his siesta and recognition showed.

"Hiya-a-a, there!" It was Hinga's usual greeting, for any- one, and Kelly had expected to hear it. The words always were spoken flatly, without enthusiasm, in Uncle John's re- strained way. Hinga stayed where he was, looking at Kelly, until he had worked his boots on, then he walked over and gave Kelly a short handshake.

Kelly smiled and shook with him, seeing that Uncle John's mouth endeavored to pull an Indian kind of sparse grin beneath the cover of his heavy drooping mustache.

Kelly said, "How are you, Uncle John?" and Hinga said, "All right, all right," with medium heartiness, and backed off.

There never had been any show of sentiment between them. In the earlier time, Kelly had been uncertain whether Uncle John had considered his presence a help or a nuisance, during the six years his uncle had "raised the orphan," as others called it. Hinga had given him the shed room to sleep in, food to eat, a man's chores to do, time in between for intermittent schooling, and, occasionally, a grudging amount of change to spend if the occasion was special enough. Hinga was not noted for being freehanded with money, but he was considered a basic fixture with roots long in the country, one who had helped to wrest it from Comanches and Mexicans; a man of solid integrity, and in matters of conflict, nobody to try to back down.

A moment of silence ensued, awkward for both.

The circumstance of Saul's departure from Uncle John and Grande Flat six years ago hung in the background of the room like the dust and the horse-pen smell and the flies. Not that there had been a row over it, and Saul had not run away in the night. He simply had collected his few possessions and informed Uncle John one day that he was riding out. Hinga had curtly asked him where he thought he was going and Saul, not knowing, had only mumbled, "I just thought I'd look around a little." There was a world to see and savor, out somewhere beyond that remote sea of monotony, but he had not known how to express this to Uncle John.

He had done enough horse-breaking and coyote-trapping jobs to pay out the horse, saddle, and rifle. With just those and his blanket roll and a saved ten dollars, he had ridden out of Grande Flat. By then he had turned twenty, ap-

13

proaching the important age when they said you were a man under the law and free to circulate.

There had been nobody else to say farewells to, unless it was Blackie Toyah and Ren Blankenship and the Mexican kid, Alice Mendoza. He had later thought of another girl, Connie Wendel, but she was little more than a child and her family owned the big store and were as remote from the pen boy as God. He had been only the Kelly boy, John Hinga's orphan nephew, and nobody who cut much of a figure. About all that Grande Flat had later meant to him in memory was a kind of constant loneliness, hard work by day, and the nightly refuge of his private boy's world and the books discovered in the shed room.

Hinga said, "You've been gone a while. Get your belly full of lookin' around?"

Kelly smiled and shrugged, as if to admit that Uncle John had a point of some kind. "Just thought I'd pay you a little visit."

Hinga eased himself with one elbow to the office counter. He had a short coughing spell and his face flushed. When he recovered, he asked, "Got a little decoration there, haven't you?"

Kelly nodded, his smile gone.

"What whittled you up?"

"Oh, I was going through a fence careless."

Hinga was one to keep his own counsel and expected others to keep theirs. He had asked all that was going to be asked. He chopped off the past six years in favor of the present by working his big watch out of his vest pocket. The hour established, he put it back and asked, "You ate yet?"

The greetings were over and now it was as if Kelly had been only across the street on an errand.

"I can go to the cafe."

"We've got grub on the stove. Nita can fix you something."

"She's new, isn't she? What became of Señora Mendoza?"

"She quit a year or two back."

Kelly inquired casually, "And her girl, Alice?"

"She grew up, teaches the Mex school kids."

He might as well ask now, Kelly thought, and found a place in his uncle's silence to put the question:

"Uncle—did you write me a note recently?"

Hinga gave him a blank look. "No. Never was one to write. Never knew where you were. Why?"

"Nothing. Just asked."

It had been unlikely, but it had seemed the place to start. There were not many in Grande Flat who would have been interested enough, one way or the other. As much of a puzzler as anything, was who had known where to address him.

The front screen opened and a man with straggly grey hair and a troubled mouth pucker padded in. He glanced at the two, spoke shortly, and familiarily headed toward a rocking chair. Kelly recognized him and said, "Hello, Doc Rice."

Hinga grunted, "You know this feller, Doc?"

The doctor altered his course to come closer. He squinted over his spectacles. "It's Kelly, isn't it?"

They shook hands and Doc Rice spoke the conventional things. He was one of a few privileged o'd-timers who habitual'y came to that room to just sit or to play dominoes or pass the range gossip with Uncle John.

Rice commented, "By gad, he turned into a big 'un, didn't he? Looks prosperous, too. Where'd he come from?"

Hinga said to Kelly, "You go on back and tell Nita to fix you some grub."

Rice turned to inspect Hinga. "How you feeling, John?"

"I feel all right," Hinga said, testily.

The doctor surveyed Kelly again. "Don't remember that little slice you got—" and almost said "boy," as he once would have, but changed it to, "Kelly."

Hinga said, "He run under a low bob wire," and chuckled.

Before he reached the washstand at the end of the hall, Kelly heard Rice comment, "Time flies, doesn't it? Where's he been?"

"Various places, I reckon," replied Hinga. "Just rode by to see me."

"He was a quiet boy, I remember. Didn't get into devilment—"

Doc Rice moved on after a time, to the Texas Bar. He asked for a glass of beer and sat in his usual location by an open window. Ren Blankenship, the manager, a moon-faced man with balding scalp, walked over heavy-footed and sat across the table. He lazily fished a pocket, found a cigar, and absently worked it in his wet lips without firing it. Rice was the only customer.

"What's going on?" Ren Blankenship asked, an idle question, for Ren knew as well as Doc Rice that there was never anything going on in Grande Flat on Mondays.

They made desultory talk as Doc Rice sipped his beer.

Ren said, "Heard the Mex fell off a wagon or something."

"Mendoza? Yes, a freight wagon turned over. Broke his leg."

"He's having a run of trouble lately."

"More than his share. He's a good Mexican."

"Hell, they ain't no such thing."

Rice shrugged. Ren asked. "What does Mendoza have to say about it?"

"He hasn't said anything, to me."

"That's the trouble. You never know what a damned greaser is *thinkin'*."

"Right now, I reckon Mendoza is thinking he's got a broken leg."

Ren chewed his cigar and said blandly, "Imagine a Mex setting himself up in business like a white man. He even landed the Army wood-hauling contract. Ain't that just like a bunch of Yankees off somewhere, dealing with a Mexican?"

"Well, you can give him credit. He's built up a profitable freighting business."

Ren put his indoor white hands and thick wrists in a

16

comfortable lock behind his head. "You ever see much of his daughter, Alice Mendoza?"

"What'd you mean, do I see much of her?"

"Nothing special. I tried to get her in the back room one time and she vamoosed like a roadrunner."

"She's smart."

"Hell, I knew her when she was a kid. You know how us boys used to chase them little brown-belly *muchachas* down on the creek." Ren ran an idea around and asked genially, "You ever seen her all over, Doc? I bet you have."

"Not many around here I haven't, in all this time. Not much difference."

"The hell they ain't. You lucky bastard." Ren grinned wetly. "I got in the wrong business."

"Alice educated herself a few cuts beyond you, Ren. Which wouldn't have to be much." Rice stood and said irritably, "You're too damned lardy. Ought to work off some of that fat."

"Doc, I was born lazy and like it the way I am."

As if he had just thought of it, Rice paused to say: "You know the Kelly boy is back? John Hinga's nephew?"

The cigar ceased wobbling. Ren Blankenship closed one eye as he squinted upward. "Saul Kelly?"

"Yeah. I said 'boy,' only he's not, of course. He's a man, now. Right sizable one. You-all used to chum together some when you were kids, I remember. You and Saul and Blackie Toyah."

Ren slowly took the cigar from his mouth and brought his chair down to its front legs. "Why, yeah, a little—What's he doin' back?"

"Just dropped in to see his uncle, I guess."

Rice departed and Ren braced his arm on the table and examined the soggy pulp of the end of his cigar. Then he stood and moved to the window, absently looked out, and came back and sat down. In a minute he called over to the dozing barkeeper: "Joe, you seen Blackie Toyah around lately?"

17

Joe mumbled he hadn't, and Ren stood again and rolled down his sleeves. He pushed through the swinging doors and sat again, in a chair against the wall on the plank walk. He saw a wagon approaching in the street. Two horsemen kept pace with it but to one side out of the dust. He watched the wagon pull up to Otto Wendel's City Mercantile. Joe, the barkeep, who had come to laze with his arms folded across the batwings, said bleakly, "McQuails in for a load of feed."

"Yeah. That's their man Strawn driving the wagon. Bert and Shep just came along to wet their whistles. Probably slipped off from the old man—he thinks nobody ought to come to town except it's Saturday."

Joe mumbled, "Hard bunch, if there ever was one. Got so I dread Saturdays."

Ren said petutantly, "Oh, I dunno. I get along with Bert and Shep all right. McQuails are a big outfit—"

"Mean bastards," Joe muttered, and padded back behind the bar.

Saul Kelly started out of the pen carrying his saddlebags, booted Winchester, and bedroll, but Uncle John appeared at the gate and motioned. "Put your stuff yonder in the shed. Where you used to bunk."

Kelly stared in surprise. "What about the boy?"

"He can sleep at home. His folks live yonder by the cattle pens."

"Hate to crowd him out," Kelly said coolly. There were four small rooms in the main building fitted out like hotel rooms, and all through the years Uncle John had maintained them for rental to the occasional overnight transients. It was plain that he was not going to splurge the use of a one-dollar room on his returned nephew.

Kelly stalked to the shed, kicked open the crookedly-hanging door, and dumped his gear to the floor. Home, all right. Uncle John was making it a point to put him back exactly where he had started. Kelly grinned to himself but there were hard knots in his jaws.

When he came to the front room, Uncle John looked at his watch and then walked behind the counter.

"About time a feller was showing up out at his place," he said vaguely. "Got to make a little ride." Kelly saw him open a drawer, fish out something that gave a metallic shine, and fumble at pinning it to his vest. Then he took a gun belt and weighted holster from another drawer and began to unroll it.

"You still a deputy, Uncle?"

"Still am. When there's something to do. Which is not much more now than it ever was. Maybe once a month something comes up from the sheriff, papers to serve or something."

Kelly remembered the times when he had been told to ride with Uncle John on some errand of the law. Usually he had done no more than hold the horses. On occasions, Uncle John had given him a deputy's badge and told him to wear it, and once or twice he had lent him a gun to pack, when Kelly was older and if the errand might involve making an arrest of a Mexican. He never had been comfortable on those occasions. He would sit his horse in the background, feeling conspicuous with the star and gun on, while Uncle John stalked into a Mexican shack or ran down some cowhand at a corral, to have a talk. This usually ended with the involved one agreeing to ride to Kiowa City in a day or two, as soon as work let up, and report to the sheriff. There never had been any physical violence, in Kelly's time.

As if he remembered also, Hinga turned back to the drawer. He tossed across a heavy nickel star matching his own. "Might as well put that on and ride with me. Like old times, huh? Not going far."

Kelly hesitated, then reluctantly pinned the star on his shirt.

"Where to?"

"Got a paper to serve on a feller. Horse stealin' complaint, only he will claim he just bought it on credit and means to pay. Might be the way it is, too. I'll decide after

19

I talk to him. Kiowa City sends this business up to me and I usually handle it the way I see it."

In the pen, as they saddled, Hinga said, "You'll know this feller. He's Blackie Toyah. Runs a sheep lease over west of town, for a bunch named McQuail. They run cattle on the range to the east, big outfit. They're new around here. Wasn't you and Blackie Toyah and Ren Blankenship all kids together?"

2.

A wagon was turning in the street at Otto Wendel's store. Two men were leading their horses diagonally across toward the Texas Bar. They paused in the street as Hinga and Kelly approached. Hinga stopped and said, "Hiya-a-a, there. Bert—Shep." The two said, "Hi-ya, John."

Kelly saw that the older one had a face that was all rock slab, big in its flat bone planes to fit the rest of his mighty body. The younger was a leaner, narrow-eyed copy of his brother.

The wagon had gone to the front of the saloon. The driver swung down there, glancing back. Another man got up from a chair in the shade of the porch, and Kelly recognized Ren Blankenship. Hinga did not bother to introduce him to the big-featured, thick-browed pair in the street. The two idly talking with Uncle John glanced toward the saloon and the younger said, with peculiar belligerence, "C'mon, Bert. Strawn's waiting for us to have a drink."

Hinga's tone changed, delaying them. "Bert, I got to serve a warrant on Blackie. I wish you and Shep would try to keep him straightened out."

Bert fixed a narrowed stare on the older man. It turned unfriendly as he asked flatly: "What's Blackie done?"

"Some dispute over whether he stole a horse or took it in pay."

Bert made a riled jerk of his broad jaw at Kelly in the background. "That the man complainin'?"

"No, not him. A feller over at North Arroyo. He claims Blackie took off with his horse and Blackie'll probably say it was part of a trade or something. The sheriff sent up the complaint. Seeing that Blackie runs sheep for you on the shares, I thought you might caution him about the way he gets into these danged scrapes."

"You aimin' to arrest him? That what you drivin' at?"

"Not if he acts right about it. He can straighten out the dispute with the man, or go down and see the sheriff and make a bond if he wants to contest it."

"Would waste a lot of time." The casual street-talk tone had gone out of Bert McQuail's voice. "Hinga, it appears to me you try to ride Blackie a little hard, that maybe because you've been around here a long time you kinda think you're Mister It. Well, we don't like any of our outfit being hounded by any amateur law or anybody else."

"Nobody's houndin' anybody," Hinga said mildly. "Blackie's just disposed to foolish trouble, and when a warrant gets sent up here, I got no choice but to serve it."

Kelly waited. He expected to see the return of common civility to the McQuails, some kind of sensible concession from Bert. But none came.

Bert slapped his bridle reins with his heavy hands. The younger, Shep, impatiently turned and snapped a one-word obscenity and started for the saloon. Bert muttered, "We'll see about this." He jerked roughly on the bridle reins and strode after Shep. Kelly saw a red flush show on Hinga's face. His uncle momentarily pressed his fist against his chest, then reined his horse about. Kelly caught up and they rode west on the cross street.

They had covered a block before Hinga spoke. "Those are Brack McQuail's boys. Bert and Shep. Brack's a hard one and he's took pains to raise them two the same way."

"So I made out."

"Shep, he's gonna marry one of Otto Wendel's daughters, the baby, Connie. So I hear. Funny match."

22

"Damn sure is," Kelly agreed. "As I remember, their mother was raising them under glass."

"Older one, Clarice, she married the feller that worked in Wendel's store. Jeb Mott. He hit here ambitious, married his boss' daughter, and practically runs things now." Hinga added gruffly, "They been tryin' to buy me out. This Mott is hell-bent to own things."

Hinga kicked his horse ahead. Habit was old within Kelly and he asked his uncle for no more than Hinga seemed inclined to convey. At the west edge of town, Hinga angled to the left at a fork in the wagon road. "I'll stop by and see Ferd Mendoza. He got a leg broke when a freight wagon turned over." He added glumly, "Thinks somebody tampered with it."

Mention of Mendoza caused Kelly to visualize the young girl he had known. He remembered that Ferd Mendoza was said to have been New Orleans Spanish blood, not greaser; but in that land they were all catalogued with the greasers. The woman, Maria, had been the station cook and housekeeper and nearest to the role of a motherly friend when the orphan kid had lived at Uncle John's. He asked, "Whatever became of Maria?"

"Ferd did well with his freighting business. Hauls supplies as far as El Paso. Time came when Maria didn't need to work any more, and Alice went to a school down at Del Rio and got educated."

His memory had already recreated the pinched features of the small, dark-skinned girl whose young body was just beginning to round out and who sometimes helped her mother in the station kitchen. And at that moment, the route of the wagon trace they followed crossed the moist trickle of a rocky cut.

Coyote Creek, it was called. In the spring the mesquites here turned thickly green and ferny, making dense shadows and hideaways along the dark banks. Kelly moved restlessly in his saddle. Covertly, he glanced northward, as if the faint image in his mind might materialize in the flesh. He saw the certain spot in the distance where the creekbed vanished

23

in a narrow bend of the bordering growth. *Coyote Creek.*
*A warm spring sundown. New grass soft on the sheltered
bank.* The meeting, unplanned—and consequences as old
as the history of youth. A young boy kindled by the strange
fire of his first fledgling knowledge of manhood; a younger
Mexican girl with thin brown body and soft, dark, trusting
eyes and hero worship in her heart; a girl suddenly no
longer a tag-along kid nuisance to be shunned and chased
away. That one truant moment of departure from their
monotonous household association—all mutual willingness
and breathless ineptness, and later a resumption of his aloofness, with their shyness compounded.

The Mendoza adobe, wagons, and sheds showed through
the mesquites. The yard was Mexican neat and the low-
roofed gallery was shaded by ancient chinaberry trees.
Hinga dismounted. "Be back in a minute." Kelly, not asked
to accompany him to the house, swung out of the saddle
and waited in the shade of a tall pin oak.

After a time, he saw her emerge at the gallery and peer
toward him. She walked down the path and he straightened
from the tree trunk and took off his hat, and knew a surprise at seeing a woman of twenty-one instead of the girl of
his memory.

Her black eyes were luminous with pleasure. Her body
was still slight but now possessed of mature curves. Her
bare legs flashed as she hurried the last distance in a swirling
play of a loosely floating cotton skirt.

"Saul Kelly!"

He advanced, matched her smile, and extended his hand.
"Alice."

She stared upward with a cocked ti!t of her dark head,
a pose he remembered. She spoke in English almost as
distinct as his own. "What a surprise! When Mr. Hinga said
you were out here—"

"Glad to see you again, Alice. I would have known you
anywhere."

24

"Not that scrawny child!" she exclaimed lightly. "Always in your way around the station."

"It was me, in your mother's way. She had to take a broom to me a few times when I was trouble in her kitchen."

"To both of us!" She flashed white teeth, her eyes shone with remembrance. "You would start the mischief and I would try to copy you."

"I can remember you sitting on the corral fence," he said. "You were the audience, watching Blackie and Ren and me practicing calf-roping or trying to break a colt. When I roped one, you would applaud."

"I thought you boys were so brave! But *you* were my big hero."

She had included the other two in her reference, the only boys he had known well in Grande Flat. But he remembered she had not liked them. They had been at an age when they dared to say bold Mexican words meant for a young girl to hear. In idle back-alley conspiracy, Blackie Toyah, obscene-minded early, had talked a scheme that they try to maneuver Alice Mendoza out to the brush. The scheme had never advanced beyond Blackie's and Ren's talk, because they were scared of the Mendozas and Uncle John and the whole adult world. Blackie was the one who had furnished the first tobacco, stolen, for their first smoking, and first to boastfully tell how it was with a girl.

A'ice gave a direct look at his thin facial knife scar, then made her attention ignore it. "You didn't even tell us goodby, Saul. I cried when *madre* came home one day and said the Kelly boy had left his Uncle John and probably was never coming back."

He smiled crookedly in a mock grimace. "Was bad manners, I'll admit. I guess I didn't think I'd be gone six years— Hear you teach the Mexican school."

"Yes. I have only ten pupils, but after there was some tax money, the county consented to let a little of it go to start our school. They needed a teacher. So I was it."

"Country's progressin'—teacher for the Mexican kids. Surprised you're not married by now."

She showed an unabashed smile. "There're not too many chances for me, you know, around Grande Flat. But you are, I take it."

"No. Never got around to it."

"Saul, I'm dying of curiosity to know all about you, where you've been, everything!"

He thought back to the long and winding sequence. "I was down in Veracruz first, happened to get a job with a mining party. New Orleans for a while, on a riverboat crew. Met another young fellow, name of Dick Hubbard, and we got to be close friends. He wanted to see over the next hill, like I did. We trailed some cattle herds up to Kansas and Wyoming. I was in Fort Worth a time, and in the Indian Territory, and in Austin—"

She searched his face with alert interest. "I could have guessed you would do that," she said firmly. "Places far away. Those books you found and always were reading. I knew it was in your blood, I think. Now I see it written on your face, the distances and places far off—Saul, your face has the look, a sort of expression—like the map of the world—" She stopped, and her gaze stayed raised in mute apology. She succeeded in keeping it from sliding off to the side of his cheek.

"I don't mind, Alice." No need to tell her he had broken the jaw of the first man who had called him *scar-face*. "If my face is going to be a map of the world, I guess it might as well show the line of the equator." He grinned to reassure her, and changed the subject. "Understand your *padre* was hurt in an accident."

A shadow crossed her features. "He is having misfortunes. And for a Mexican, you know, there is no place to turn. My mother and I want him to sell the freighting business to some men who wish to buy it. But he is stubborn about this—I do not wish to burden you with the Mendozas' troubles."

He saw Hinga emerge from the house and start down the

26

path. He had no expectations that Alice could be the one, but he would ask. "You didn't write to me recently, did you? A little note, addressed to where I was?"

"Why, no, Saul. *You* never wrote, you know, because I asked Mr. Hinga. I just never knew where you were."

He did not answer the inquiry in her expression. "Never got around to writing. But I thought of you, sometimes."

Hinga was ready to ride, and Saul said, "I'll stop by to see Ferd and Maria, first chance I get."

"Please do, Saul."

He looked back as they rode out of the clearing. She remained at the pin oak, a slight figure with her loose cotton skirt and dark hair playing in the breeze.

Hinga said, "Ferd Mendoza's built himself up a good freighting business. For a Mexican, he's done mighty well. Got four or five drivers, some good teams and wagons. Now somebody's after him. Accidents happening that ought not to happen. Threats of one kind and another. Think he knows more than he lets on—you know how a Mexican is afraid to speak up. Not much you can do for a greaser. Only way they ever can get into court is to be the defendant, accused of something. Like the niggers in East Texas."

Kelly waited, but Uncle John changed the subject. "Now, Blackie Toyah's place is a distance over yonder beyond Buffalo Draw. He'll be surprised to see you."

"I guess he will."

"He didn't improve any when he got grown."

The Toyah place had the cluttered run-down look of a typical sheep camp. The nester shabbiness was matched by the unwashed look of Blackie, who trudged up from the pens. He was a hard-knit, jerky-gaited man with dodging buckshot eyes and a gorilla hang to his swinging arms. He and Hinga traded cautious greetings, then he went into a talkative, false-ringing show of affability as he and Kelly spoke the conventional words of seeing each other again. This soon played out and the talk bogged as the men rested on the porch edge.

A string-haired, wind-reddened woman came barefooted

27

to the dogtrot doorway. Mrs. Toyah saw the law badges and snapped a blunt, "What's this damn' posse for, Blackie?"

"Social call, honey."

"Trouble call you mean!" she said stridently. "You *ride* him, John Hinga. If I was you, Blackie, I'd take the shotgun and run these two off the place! You got the McQuails to back you—"

Blackie snarled, "Shut up! Get on back in the house." She retreated, grumbling. Blackie said, "Damn woman. Always buttin' in. Now, John, I reckon I know what you're here for." He hooked a crafty squint on Hinga and his words flowed like slick sheep through a chute. "That sonofabitch claims I took his horse, don't he? Well, he owed me on a wood trade, and when you deal with a cheatin' sonofabitch like him you got to collect the best way you can—ain't that right? You know Mack Feeney, never paid a nickel he didn't have to—white trash out of East Texas—what's he claimin', John? That I *stole* his horse?"

Hinga said it appeared that way, that Feeney had sworn out a complaint in Kiowa City and he thought Blackie had better make a trip down to see the sheriff. Or else send the horse back and try to straighten out the issue with Feeney.

"Ain't got time!" Blackie protested. "Hell, you know how busy we are, this time of year. Bert and Shep McQuail ain't gonna like this. John, you made it a little rough on me that last time, and Bert and Shep, they said next time anybody come along and tried to interfere with my work, by God to tell 'em to come see *them*. Don't mean you no trouble, but I work for the McQuails on this lease and damned if I ain't about a mind to do just that—somebody wants to make trouble over that sorry horse, damn horse that's mine legal, think I'll just say, 'you go brace Bert McQuail, mister, I ain't a-stirrin' a peg till the McQuails say—' "

"Got no warrant for Bert or Shep," said Hinga patiently. "I just got a warrant for Blackie Toyah." Then Hinga stood and said, "You be thinking about it. Where is the horse? Down yonder in the pen? Think I'll go down and see what the blame horse looks like—" He stalked off toward the corral.

Kelly waited uncomfortably, remembering well how Blackie would always defend himself, and the boyish crafty schemes he often hatched up in the monotonous horse-pen-and-alley days of Grande Flat's slow-dragging summers. Painfully, he remembered Blackie's plot that had been the most grandiose of them all, and the days of his terror that had resulted.

As if the same recollection occurred to him, Blackie turned for a hard stare at Kelly. He lowered his voice.

"What'd you come back here for, Kelly?"

"Just a visit."

"You know to keep your mouth shut, don't you?"

"Don't worry, Blackie."

"You ain't gone off and got to thinkin' you ought to spill the beans or something, have you?"

"Nothing like that. It's all past and forgotten."

"Well, by God, it can still make me nervous. Will make Ren Blankenship nervous, too."

"The time's long past," said Kelly with finality. "Surprised you're still worried."

"By God you might be worried, too, if you had to stay here and knew old Clabe Peabody lived with his shotgun loaded for the day he might find out! Listen, you better remember me and Ren could make up a story that you was in it, too—"

"That threat you made before. It never bothered me, doesn't now."

Blackie said glumly, "I still don't feel good, you knowin'—"

"I kept my mouth shut and my decision was my own. We were just kids, and I guess I felt more loyalty to you and Ren than I did to something called 'the law.' Anyhow, nobody's answerable now. The statute of limitation—the time the law could have done anything is long since passed."

"That's what they *say!* Well, I wouldn't trust any of those

29

bastards down at the courthouse just on *say*. Anyhow, they ain't no statute passed out for old Clabe Peabody and his shotgun. Won't be till he's dead. He near went crazy, trying to find out who killed his brother."

"It was a bad thing, Blackie. It's stayed with me. I was the one that knew you and Ren pulled it."

"Hell, yes, it was bad! Damn it, I know it was bad. Just an accident, that's all. My gun just went off accidental."

Kelly remembered his own hours of torment following the discovery of Pete Peabody's corpse hanging off the runaway wagon. He looked coldly into the distance. "What two sixteen-year-old boys did a long time ago is forgotten, as much as I can make it forgotten. You stewed the big idea. You tried to talk me and Ren into it for weeks. You were bitten with the bandit bug. It damn near sounded good. An easy way to grab the big money you thought he carried. But I didn't like it, Blackie." He added bluntly, "I reckon because I didn't much like you then, actually."

"Don't make a goddam to me!" Blackie retorted.

Kelly grinned without the grin showing in the steady look he fastened on the sweat-streaked man beside him. "Thinking back, I know it was the pure boredom of the town, the itch we had for wanting to do something exciting. Even to playing bandits. You said all Ren and I would have to do was stay back and keep a lookout on the road that night, that you knew how to do the rest and nobody would get hurt and we would make some money. You almost sold me, Blackie."

"You didn't have the guts!" Blackie snarled.

"Maybe that was it. For months I was as scared as you and Ren, because I was the one who *knew* who had done it. Every able-bodied man in the country hunting the bandits—"

"The gun went off accidental. I told you a million times."

Kelly vividly recalled how Ren had reluctantly yielded to the dare after Blackie's glib persuasion. Ren had agreed to join him as the "lookout" and had not seen the actual shooting. Both boys had fled in the night. Terrified for weeks,

30

Ren and Kelly had listened to Blackie doggedly defend himself. He had related that Peabody had only laughed at the masked boy's demand and denied that he carried money, and Blackie's insistence that his gun happened to go off, that he had not meant to shoot.

Blackie said sourly, "I don't much like you back here, Kelly, it'll make Ren skittish all over again. He's *still* scared."

"Not what I came back for." Kelly stood. "Maybe I did right or maybe I did wrong, protecting you. But you and Ren were nearest thing to friends I had here. So as far as I'm concerned, it's past and forgotten."

John Hinga came upgrade, puffing for breath.

"Not a bad-looking horse," he commented. "Blackie, I don't know how else to handle this. I'd like for you to ride in with me and we can fix up a bond, something to satisfy 'em down at the sheriff's office. I'll do it soon as we get back and you can get the McQuails or Ren Blankenship or somebody to sign it."

Blackie complained that it was a lot of trouble over nothing, but in the end he conceded that there wasn't much else Hinga could do. Kelly silently listened to their discussion, remembering Uncle John's informal approach to law matters in the community where he knew everyone and handled such things in the accommodating way of the land. Hinga stalked alone out in the yard while Blackie went to the pen to saddle the horse in question. Blackie called to his wife that he was riding to town and to shut her mouth when she began a harangue against John Hinga.

The three rode southeast on the wagon tracks and had reached the sandy floor of Buffalo Draw when Uncle John, riding ahead, pulled up. Kelly and Blackie pulled up, too, thinking Hinga was intending to say something. The sun had dropped below the rock rim high above but dusk had not settled, and they could see that Hinga's features appeared contorted.

Uncle John pushed his fist to his chest. He said, "Saul— Blackie—"and then Kelly saw him sway sideways in his saddle. He kept his fist knotted to his chest. His other hand dropped the reins. Kelly called, "You sick?" and kicked his horse forward, but not in time.

Uncle John bent and rolled out of his saddle. His feet came free of the stirrups as he fell on his shoulders. The horse curved itself and sidestepped away from where Hinga lay in the dry gravel. When Kelly and Blackie swung off and ran to him, he was crumpled on his side, his arms limp and his body still.

They tried to straighten him. Kelly listened for a heart-beat and could hear none.

They passed an awed stare between them as they balanced over Uncle John on their bootheels, and then both looked down again at the face already gray.

"Well, I'll be—!" Blackie muttered.

"I think he's dead." Kelly had trouble forming the word with his dry tongue. "Just like that—!"

Blackie said, "Be damn!"

"Blackie, get his horse. I'm nearly positive, but we ought to hurry him in to Doc Rice—there might be—"

They worked at lifting Uncle John in a limp face-down droop across his saddle. The horse showed its dislike for that, but they calmed it, and started for town with Blackie leading the reins and Kelly riding alongside to steady the body. By the time they reached the outskirts, they knew there was no hurry. Nothing for Doc Rice to do now. John Hinga was dead.

When they turned into the first town street, Blackie slowed his horse. "Kelly, before we get in there, why don't you take off that damn silly badge? You ain't any more of a deputy than I am, and it'll make me look funny." He jerked a nod toward the body across the saddle. "He's gone, and we might as well forget the whole damned business about me and Feeney's damned horse—"

Kelly looked at him blankly. Blackie raised his voice in harsh insistence. "Dammit, do like I told you—take off that goddam badge! No use for a crowd to collect and think I'm under arrest or somethin'—Now you ain't aimin' to try to act like no damn lawman, are you? You got enough to do, with just him—"

It didn't seem to Kelly to matter. He felt stunned. Death had dipped its wings in the stillness back in Buffalo Draw, out of nowhere. A bold and awesome visit, more shaking to a man than if it had come violently, because it was so quietly done. Thinking of other things, he reached to unpin the badge as an unimportant small favor to Blackie. But Blackie, in his fevered agitation, spoke again, too quickly and too much like Blackie Toyah. "Just remember you ain't no law, so don't try to make it I'm under arrest." He laughed derisively. "Hell, that would be a joke, wouldn't it —*you* tryin' to arrest *me! My scar-faced old compadre!*"

Kelly's hand dropped from the badge.

"Get the reins. Lead the horse to the station while I steady his body."

Blackie hesitated, but after one look at Kelly he scowled and caught up the reins again. They paraded slowly to the station. Word passed on the street as they went by, and when they stopped at the back of the building men began to gather on foot. Other hands lifted Uncle John from his horse. Doc Rice appeared, made an examination, and straightened. He shook his head.

"Not unexpected. I'd warned him. Was his heart." He snapped his fingers once, to illustrate.

In response to somebody's low-voiced question, he said, "Saul Kelly—his nephew."

A few of the men remembered Kelly. They came over and somberly spoke and two or three shook his hand. They were men he dimly remembered, and they once had called him "the Kelly boy," but now they said just "Kelly."

They spoke and had their look at the stranger's tall and hardened frame, the map-of-the-world face with its weather lines and the long, thin scar, the gun, the deputy's badge still pinned on his shirt. Then the group yielded ground as three newcomers pushed through.

Kelly recognized the two McQuails and their wagon driver, Strawn. From where he stood at the pen rails he heard the question, somebody's sober reply, "Heart failure," and then the McQuails saw Blackie.

Bert asked sharply, "What happened out there?"

"Nothing," Blackie said. "We were just ridin' in, me and him and Saul Kelly, there. Little to-do over a horse. He wanted me to sign something. Then he keeled over, right there in Buffalo Draw. Was all over in a minute."

The gathering shuffled awkwardly, looking down at death at their feet in the curiosity men will show for one of themselves newly become a corpse.

Bert McQuail said, "Well, you come on with us, Blackie. Old Mister It hasn't got any need for you now."

Blackie mumbled, "All right, Bert," and reached for his bridle reins. He dragged a speculative look to Kelly. Kelly straightened from the fence rails.

He tallied the oversized bulk of Bert McQuail and felt the sensitive prod of an abiding dislike, already formed.

"He's got a bond to sign before he leaves, McQuail. Charge of horse stealing."

The men stopped their low talk and shifted uneasily. Doc Rice worriedly peered over his spectacles at one man then another. Jonesy the oak-armed smithy, mumbled, "Now, lookee here—" Kelly turned to Blackie, his boyhood friend who had never quite been a friend, only a dismal straw of companionship to clutch in Grande Flat's long days of monotony. He said, "You're still under arrest, Blackie."

He had not felt that he owed much to Uncle John, but he owed even less to Blackie Toyah. This was a small account for John Hinga, a shabby final thing, unasked for but passed on to his hands, in a way, when Uncle John had tossed the badge to him. Somehow, it would seem unfitting if he turned his back on it in this moment of inherited purpose unfinished.

Bert McQuail took three weighty steps toward him, a man publicly challenged and proud to meet it.

"Who's the scar-face with the badge?"

Somebody answered, "Why he's Hinga's nephew, Bert. The Kelly, er—feller."

Bert snapped, "You a deputy?"

Kelly said slowly, "Not exactly—"

" 'Not exactly!' What kind of a goddam answer is that? Blackie, come on!"

Kelly began a half turn toward Blackie, not certain in his mind what he meant to do or say. The issue seemed lacking propriety, with John Hinga dead at their feet. The dark-garbed figure of Strawn drifted snake-smooth into view at the corner of his eye. Strawn with his eyes dead and his long fingers resting over his gun holster. Bert saw him, too, and muttered, "Never mind, I can handle him—"

Someone barked in agitation, "Hey, don't pull that—!"

Yet Strawn kept his gun butt caressed as if by compulsion and held his cloudy gaze invitingly on Kelly. His lips stretched thin. He murmured, "Your move, deputy."

Blackie pulled on the reins and walked past, leading the horse. He said tautly, "Hell, no cause for trouble. I'll come back tomorrow or sometime, fix up the papers—" He walked on and Kelly hardly gave him notice. He was moving toward Strawn, so imperceptibly that his movement almost was unnoticed as the crowd shuffled about. He brushed past the solid bulk of Bert McQuail who had half-faced around to follow Blackie.

Strawn had held his position, near Shep McQuail, and his right hand still hung down to his gun, and his left was down too, and rigid, and did him no good. Kelly's move, when he made it, erupted in a streak of speed and shoulder power from timed thrust of leg muscle, and nobody who was looking had ever seen a man in Grande Flat get hit so hard.

The crack of Kelly's fist to Strawn's jaw made a sound like a brittle board snapping; and the men saw an unusual damaging refinement to a fist blow, the way Kelly's fist hit and still plowed upward, all in the same impact, taking hide and hurt with it clear to Strawn's eye. Strawn seemed dynamited off the ground and to fall backward for several prolonged seconds. Men collided with each other to make falling room. His skull smashed the earth and bounced. Strawn made brief convulsive twistings, then gave up trying.

Kelly already had turned to face Bert McQuail.

"He said it was my move. Now I guess it's yours."

Bert had trouble tearing his opened-mouth gaze off Strawn. He said hoarsely, "Kelly, I'm gonna take you apart—"

"He made a mistake. Don't you make one, too. Tell him never to offer to pull a gun on me unless he's prepared to go through with it."

Men came to life and the muscular force of them crushed in between Kelly and the two McQuails.

"Here, now," the blacksmith roared, "let's break this up—!"

"There's a dead man here—"

"Kelly—Bert—everybody cool off—"

Doc Rice raised a voice of authority. "We've got a few things to do. Some of you get a hold of John Hinga and carry him in the house. Somebody go tell the undertaker, and somebody better inform the preacher. Rest of you just pull out."

Kelly turned his back on the two McQuails and the men pressed in between, and on Blackie Toyah who again started for the street, leading the horse. Kelly bent with three other men, two on each side, and they carried Uncle John's body into the rear of the stage building. One of the men, grunting with the exertion, spoke advice intended to be helpful. "You'd do well, Kelly, to stay inside awhile, till Strawn comes to and they fetch him off somewhere."

They all wanted to be helpful. One said he would tell the undertaker to come get John's body, and another said he would pass the word along to the preacher and the church ladies.

3.

The word of Hinga's departure and Kelly's return winged from house to house in the early evening and made supper conversation. Deaths were rare in Grande Flat, and births, too, for that matter; the town somehow never had been much of a place for starting a life or concluding one.

This evening, the people had something new to talk about. They spoke of small things about John Hinga's time on earth and Saul Kelly's time as his uncle's pen boy. Doc Rice's wife already had heard about John Hinga, and when the doctor came to supper he needed to supply only a few words of detail. She had heard about the other incident, too, and asked if it were true that the Kelly boy had knocked down one of the McQuail men.

"The Kelly man," Doc Rice corrected. "Yeah. He hit that feller from Kansas hard enough to put him out for fifteen minutes."

She looked steadily at her husband and said, "That was not wise, was it?"

He nodded grudgingly. "He doesn't know Strawn or the McQuails. They moved in since he left."

For nearly forty years she had seen him withdraw to brief moods of silence following a death, and she knew to permit him to eat with his private thoughts uninterrupted. Only once did he react any differently or say anything unusual in regard to this particular passing of a life. She heard his comment, knew that she did not rightly understand him, and made no comment.

"All these years," he said, "I've resisted any temptation to play God in situations that come to a doctor and leave things to Somebody better prepared to take over from where I left off." She could not tell whether he was talking to her or himself. He pulled out his pipe and tobacco and seemed to be addressing the filling job. "One time I guess I've slipped. Knew blamed well I was, when I did it."

He picked up his bag and his hat, saying he would be at his office or in the saloon or at the stage station, and trudged back the two blocks to town. He intended to stop by the station where he customarily left his bag on evenings when he did not want to climb the stairs to his office farther down the street.

Saul Kelly had decided to sleep in the main house after all and had moved his gear into one of the small rent rooms. He had the passing feeling of guilt that he owed Uncle John the dollar rate. He changed to fresh clothes, leaving off the deputy badge. He found a linament and soaked it into his bruised right-hand knuckles. Nita, the cook, stoic to the tragedy, informed him that there was food on the stove, and departed for her home. Jimmie, the pen boy, came, almost inarticulate in the circumstance of sudden death. Kelly asked him to proceed with the usual evening chores. He had one concern, and Jimmie answered by saying that the weekly stage-runs, north and south, were not due until Thursday and Friday.

Kelly had just entered the front room when Ren Blankenship walked in. They were the same age, nearing twenty-seven, but Ren looked older with his balding head, brown facial splotches, and flabbiness. Ren chewed a cigar, his handshake was limp, and they talked with surface affability underlaced with reserve.

Ren said, after the preliminaries, "Sorry to hear about the trouble."

"It was sudden. Doc Rice said he'd been having heart pains."

Ren shook his head. "That, too. But I was referrin' to you and the McQuails. Strawn's a fast gun—a killer. The McQuails picked him up in Kansas or somewhere."

Kelly asked shortly, "How long ago?"

"Oh, couple of years. On one of their market drives. They—"

"They drove to Kansas? Last year?"

"Yeah. And the year before. Saul, you—"

"What place in Kansas?"

"Hell, I think it was Abilene. Anyhow, what I'm sayin, you monkey with them and you not only got Strawn down on you. You got Bert and Shep and the whole bunch. Bert's hot-tempered and nobody ever heard of a man that ever licked him. Why didn't you leave Blackie alone?"

Kelly asked curiously, "Understand you run the saloon. You own it?"

"No. The manager. Jeb Mott owns it. He married Clarice, Otto Wendel's daughter. Runs Wendel's store for him. You remember them two little Wendel girls, the way their folks never would let 'em mix with anybody. Especially anybody like you and me and Blackie." Ren grinned lazily in reminiscence. "You know how we used to talk how we'd like the chance to get 'em off somewhere and mess up them nice curls and starched dresses. Well, this Jeb Mott hit here and turned out the one that got to mess up Clarice. The younger one, Connie, she's due to marry Shep McQuail. That lucky bastard will be the first one to take that delicate china doll out of wrappings."

This was about the last prospect, and not much of one, but Kelly asked quietly: "Ren, did you ever write a note to me, anywhere?"

"Me write? Never even heard of you after you skipped. Me and Blackie were glad to be shed of you. You know why."

Doc Rice came in then, and Ren said, "Come down and have a drink on me, Kelly. You aim to be here long?"

"Just a few days."

Kelly and Rice sat for a while making a limping conversation. Rice revealed that Hinga had complained of chest pains several times, for months. "I figured it was his heart and told him so, but he wouldn't have any truck with the idea."

This gave Kelly a small glimmer of possibility, but it turned out short-lived.

"If you thought this might happen, Doc, did it occur to you that maybe I should be brought back?"

"Can't say as it did."

"Doc, did you happen to write me a note of any kind recently?"

Rice peered at him over his spectacles. "Nope. What kind of note?"

"It said—" Kelly decided that he could trust Doc Rice. He took out his wallet and unfolded a small sheet of paper. "This note." Doc Rice read the thinly printed pencil lettering:

IF YOU RETURN YOU MIGHT FIND INFORMATION OF INTEREST CONCERNING WHAT HAPPENED AT ARBUCKLE CANYON.

He passed it back to Kelly and shook his head. "What does it mean?"

"It came to me at—where I was. Someone knew where to address me."

"Kelly, just where in the hell *have* you been? What do you do?"

"I've done several things, Doc. For the last year, I've—well, I've worn this—"

He drew a small silver shield from his pocket and extended it.

Doc Rice looked closely. "Well, I'll be damn." He squinted a new appraisal over Kelly. "Deputy United States Marshal, huh? Where?"

"Right now I'm in charge of the Austin district."

"State capital, eh?" Rice thought of something and chuckled. "And Bert McQuail questioned your right to wear a country lawman's badge! That's a good one."

"This is confidential, Doc. Mostly, I work undercover.

40

The people out here don't know that and I'd as soon it stayed that way."

Rice pursed his lips. "What's that about Arbuckle Canyon?"

Kelly hesitated. Then he touched his cheek. "It has to do with this. And the loss of three thousand dollars. And the murder of my best friend, a man named Richard Hubbard. It's a place in the Arbuckle mountains in Indian Territory."

Rice waited. Kelly intended to say no more. Thoughtfully, Rice said, "Richard Hubbard. Same name as the Governor of Texas."

Kelly said quietly: "Dick was his son. He and I met a long time ago on an exploration expedition down in Mexico. We were like brothers, ever after that. We made the trail drives together, saw the country. His father came to be like *my* father."

Rice whistled softly. "Long way from that shed room back yonder in the pen to the Governor's mansion in Austin."

Kelly smiled thinly. "It sure is. Dickie and I stayed there many a time, in between travels to somewhere."

Rice asked curiously, "Just what happened up there in the Arbuckles?"

"We were coming home with cattle-sale money, just Dick Hubbard and me. We got ambushed one night on the trail. Dick was killed and I got this knife slice in the melee. I rolled over a cliff and fell God knows how far in the dark, and the men who jumped us took out without trying to find me. I guess they thought I was dead, anyway. A bunch of tame Cherokees found me two days later and took care of me for a month till my ribs healed."

"It was your money?"

"No, it was a part of the herd-sale proceeds we were bringing back in cash for the herd owner. I put in a year, looking and tracing, beginning in Kansas. No clues ever panned out. I got acquainted with a few federal lawmen during that time. A year ago I was given the chance to become a U.S. Deputy Marshal." He added, "I've had other cases to work on since, but I reckon you can imagine how I've always kept this one in the front of my mind."

"So you got that note," Rice prompted.

"Came to me in Austin the other day. Postmarked Laredo, but I could only figure it must mean to come back here, to Grande Flat, and that someone took or sent it to Laredo for mailing. I thought maybe the writer would make himself known, or follow it up. Now I doubt if he will. Maybe his nerve failed, or maybe that was all he meant to offer."

Rice furrowed his brow. "Maybe he thought the tip was enough, that it would be your job to work it out when you got here."

A few townsmen entered then, and Rice said he would drift on. Saul Kelly contended with getting the names and faces of his callers straight, in the strained visiting that followed. Some of the men had brought their wives, dressed up and powdered and business-like for their roles as organizers of Grande Flat's infrequent funerals. They inspected the returned Kelly man under cover of their expressions of sympathy, asked if there was anything they could do, and the women said all the church details would be taken care of. The visitors came and went, with each call awkward and ragged talk, since there was no family to express condolences to nor heap food upon.

In a lull when the most recent visitors had departed, and Kelly was alone in the front room, a man and two women entered. The man was a stocky business type wearing a salt and pepper suit and a stickpin in his shirt. When he removed his hat, his hair showed plastered down and combed in a pair of thin wings. He had thick lips and a ruddy complexion, an air of assurance and a ready command for a situation.

"I'm Jeb Mott," he said without hesitation. "City Mercantile. I guess you're Hinga's nephew. Just paying a sympathy call. This is my wife, Clarice. That's her sister,

Connie Wendel." He stepped from in front of the two women as if raising a stage curtain. His entire interest transferred to making a roving survey of the station's front room as if listing each individual fixture. "Place sure has run down," he said.

The names "Clarice" and "Connie" reminded Kelly at once of two small girls in curls, walking together and holding hands, and of the aloof Otto Wendels who sheltered their prim small daughters from the harsher elements of Grande Flat. Clarice, not quite a delicate unwrapped china doll now, took over at once. She had become a slightly faded young woman, well dressed, with her yellow curls painstakingly arranged and pinned. The younger sister, Connie, standing in her proper place just behind her older sister, maintained a small, private, red-lipped smile as she examined the newcomer with demure interest bordering on whimsical speculation.

Saul finally was given an opening by Clarice. "You were the Wendel girls, I remember. Otto Wendel had the big store down the street. I guess we just never got acquainted."

Clarice, the spokesman, politely arranged the past. "Yes, our parents were rather strict. Jeb came here to work in the store. He's from a prominent family in Galveston. Later we were married and he's the owner now—that is, with Papa and Mama and me. Connie is the school teacher. Not that she needs to work. Jeb and I own quite a bit of property now. Let's see, you had some trouble or something here as a boy and ran away, didn't you. I vaguely remember talk, but Connie and I were just children then. Papa and Mama never would let town gossip be talked at our house."

He waited a moment, to see if Clarice had run down. "Well, it wasn't exactly like that. I just left. No trouble with Uncle John."

Clarice talked again, but somehow there was nothing in the whole room but Connie Wendel in the background, that unfathomable demure smile, a subtle long-distance invitation a man could misread but might make him speculate

43

as Blackie Toyah had speculated in the boy-talk time of the back-alley days.

He said, with an edge of reserve, conscious that Clarice dominated the surface with her words but Connie dominated all else with just her silence and luminous appraisal: "It's nice of you to come by. I would have known you both, I think, but it was a long time ago," and Clarice said coolly, "I don't know that I would have recognized you. You've changed."

Then Connie spoke for the first time. "I would have known you, Saul."

The sound of her voice, as well as her expression, spanned the years for him. Did she know that her looks secretly *dared* a man or did she just happen to smile like that?

She said, "I thought you were a most interesting boy and always wished I was old enough for you to notice."

"I noticed, Connie."

"But you hardly ever spoke to us."

"Well, I hardly ever saw you."

Her smile held on. "We were hitched to very strict parents. I would have run away to your horse pen except that Mama always was along or else I had to hold Clarice's hand when we walked to the store."

"It was those starched dresses and yellow curls that scared me. You two always looked like you were going to a party." He managed to speak easily, but the call was turning burdensome and he would be relieved when their duty was done and they had departed.

Clarice said archly, "Everyone was always telling Mother that we were too pretty to be living out here. Mother came from Galveston, the old Gulf Coast aristocracy."

He acknowledged that with a respectful nod, then Connie deftly cut the superiority out from under her sister. "I was downright envious of Alice Mendoza."

For a confused second, Kelly's mind flashed to Coyote Creek. But Connie added, "She could sit on your corral fence and watch you boys play at bronc riding, and we

44

couldn't. It was supposed to be unladylike. The Wendel sisters didn't sit on top rails where boys were."

Clarice said charitably, "Alice Mendoza has made something of-herself, for a Mexican. She teaches the children in the Mexican school. Or maybe you've already seen her."

"Yes, I've seen her."

Clarice nodded, as if that confirmed something. It confirmed that the Wendels had catalogued the Hinga pen boy with the shack greasers, at the bottom of Grande Flat's social line.

"And I teach the white school," said Connie. "Of course, they have the Mexican children properly separated from us. So there'll be no contamination."

"You're not married?"

"Oh, no."

Clarice seemed to function as her sister's interpreter. "She's practically engaged, though. To Shep McQuail. Let's see—you wouldn't know the McQuails. They're new. They own quite a large cattle range east of town and a sheep lease that Blackie Toyah runs for them. Bert and Shep have taken big herds to the Kansas market."

"I had the pleasure of meeting them today."

Jeb Mott, his exploratory circling of the big room completed, came back with a hand in his side pocket producing a sound like two silver dollars clinking. "The McQuails are my biggest customers. I reckon John Hinga always envied me for the feed business I get from them, when he didn't get any of it."

"Shep is madly in love with Connie," said Clarice.

"We want a business for Shep to run, in town," Jeb Mott said. "So Connie won't have to live out in the wilds."

"So much for my private life," Connie said flatly. "Saul isn't interested in that."

Jeb Mott cleared his throat. "Kelly, this probably isn't the time to go into it, but I'm interested in buying this property." Time or not, he proceeded to go into it. "Now I know you'll want to put Hinga's property and business on the market, so you can go on your way. I made him an offer a time or two in the past. I imagine you'll be the one to settle up his affairs, and you and me can talk business. Hinga's let the place run down, but I've got the capital to improve things and I'd be interested in taking it over, providing you don't try to hold me up on it." He grinned and winked.

"No, I guess this isn't the right time, now. In fact, I don't know anything about Uncle John's affairs or how they'll be handled."

"Well, we can bring in a lawyer," said Mott, as if the transaction already was at the closing stage. "Of course my father-in-law will have to be satisfied—Otto Wendel. But I more or less handle the business decisions and he'll follow my recommendations."

Clarice looked the room over, as Mott had. "Connie, when you and Shep are married, this would be a business we could let Shep operate and that way you could live in town—"

Connie said blandly, "Well, I don't know if they could spare him from running the ranch—"

"You come to see me," said Mott briskly. "You'll want to get this headache off your hands right away and I'm in a position to put down the cash for it."

Only Connie extended her hand to him as they moved to depart.

He said, "If it's in order, Connie, my best wishes to the future Mrs. Shep McQuail."

"It isn't settled yet. Clarice just likes to have me engaged for her own satisfaction, I think. She and Jeb are afraid I might become Grande Flat's old-maid school teacher."

"She's had plenty of chances!" Clarice said stiffly.

Jeb and Clarice moved toward the door, but Connie lingered. "I thought you might be planning to stay and run your uncle's business," she said. "But you don't look like you're meant to stay in Grande Flat. You look like you might have seen quite a bit of the world—and found it interesting."

46

Mott called back gruffly, "He'll probably be glad to sell and get out." Clarice said thinly, "Good night, Saul. Come on, Connie."

Connie delayed to explain: "Mama is visiting in Del Rio and Papa had to work at the store tonight, otherwise they would have paid you a sympathy visit, Saul."

Down the block, Mott paused across the street from the saloon and said he was going in to have a sociable drink and hear the town talk. He left the women to walk on to their homes, Clarice to the Motts' spacious whitewashed adobe, and Connie to the big gingerbread-trimmed two-story frame Wendel house centering the next full block beyond.

"Don't you want to spend the night with us," asked Clarice, "instead of being alone in that big house?"

"I've always stayed alone. I like it that way."

Clarice said thoughtfully, "Isn't it odd, for that man to come back after all this time? Maybe it's our luck. Now Jeb can make a deal for the property. He's so anxious to get it, and Mr. Hinga never would so much as discuss a sale. Jeb is sure a railroad will build through here some day."

"Jeb is always lucky."

"Isn't he? He always gets what he wants."

Connie thought grimly, *Except one time, when I was home alone*. Jeb, fired with whisky and desire, had said with vicious assurance: "There'll be another time, Connie. When I set my mind on getting something I like, I get it. You be thinking it over."

Still thinking of the property, Clarice said, "In a way, I guess it's fortunate for Jeb's plans that Mr. Hinga died."

"Oh, a small thing, if it accommodates Jeb," Clarice murmured.

"Connie, do you really remember the Kelly boy? I just barely do."

"Yes, I remember him, how he looked and what he wore —always so wonderful'y dirty, the way I wished we could get—I think I wished he would find me alone and *mess me up*—"

"Connie!"

"Oh, just a kid thought. Didn't you ever have unsterilized ideas like that?"

"I hope Mama never dreamed such a thing would enter your head."

"She wouldn't. Mama boiled our thoughts for us like she did our drinking water."

"If I were you, I'd try to have a little sense and set a wedding date with Shep. While you still have a chance to make a good catch."

"If you have any influence with Shep, I'd like for you to suggest that he take off his spurs and gunbelt the next time he tries to—to have a rehearsal before the main show."

"Connie!"

"With all that on in one small buggy, I felt like my virginity was being challenged by a hardware store."

"Connie!"

Clarice haughtily turned into her own gate and Connie slowly walked on to the big empty house in the next block. She knew an ancient weariness of a younger sister's life-long hearing the one-word condemnation, *Connie!* She also harbored from the past one small girlish puzzle in her mind. Clarice had been too intent on her plans for marrying Jeb Mott and had not seemed to notice. But Connie had known that her parents strangely had looked down on Jeb as just the store's hired man and then suddenly, the next minute, it seemed, had practically presented Jeb with their daughter, with their City Mercantile, with all their business interests. It was true there weren't many chances for a girl in Grande Flat or anywhere in that remote border country. But it had not appeared to her young mind that the prospects were *that* bad, that her parents should have worked for that match as if secretly in panic.

She went up the wide steps and entered the big house, bolted the door, and lighted the lamps in the parlor.

From the saloon, Jeb Mott went to the City Mercantile, unlocked the front door, and walked back to the office where an overhead lamp burned. His gaunt father-in-law, working on the books, raised a sour and watery glance, then bent again to his figures.

Mott took a cigar from the display case on the counter and ceremoniously put fire to it. He leaned against the counter across from Wendel and spoke with satisfaction. "I broke the ice with the Kelly man. I think I can persuade him to sell, and at my figure. I'm going to own that place sooner or later. If the railroad ever builds I'll make it into a big hotel and have me a gold mine."

Otto Wendel, age-lined and austere, slowly put down his pencil and stared at his son-in-law.

"Why don't you be content with what you've got?"

Mott flicked the ashes. "Ambition, Otto, ambition."

Wendel rubbed his hand across his face. He stared with the eyes of a trapped animal and spoke in a voice heavy with the old yeast of living hate. "You schemin' sonofabitch. You dirty, blackmailin' sonofabitch. You want everything in sight."

"Don't work yourself up, Otto."

Wendel said numbly, "I should have killed you at the beginning."

"But you didn't, Otto. Now we're all one, fine, highfalutin' family."

"Too late," the old man whispered, barely aloud.

"Yeah. And don't ever get the idea to do it. It's in writing somewhere safe, Otto. Ever' juicy detail of where the leading citizen found his high-chinned wife. Don't ever cross me, Otto. She might have to wind up back in Galveston and she's a little old to have to start her profession again where you found her." Mott chuckled. "The straitlaced Mrs. Otto Wendel!"

Wendel muttered, "Never thought I could hate a human as much as I hate you."

"That's fine, Otto." Mott clamped his teeth down on the cigar. "But outwardly, we're all love and high quality in this family. Ain't that right? Now get on with the bookkeeping. And keep it honest."

Outside, he paused on the front walk to inhale the cool

of the night. He floated an inventory glance up and down the street of window lights. The City Mercantile at his back was his proud and substantial bulwark dominating the business scene. Down the street he could see the saloon, which he already owned, and in the distance the Hinga stage station, feed supply, and horse sales business, which he would be owning as soon as he could drive a trade with the Kelly man.

He had not done bad, Mott thought with satisfaction, for a man who had landed in this country less than five years ago. It had been sheer luck, of course, stumbling on the identity of Mrs. Wendel. But he had to concede there had been an element of sharp brainwork in it, too. That, and a good memory and the hunch to trace the back trail to Galveston, and finally, the guts to use what he knew after he had nailed down the secret beyond doubt. As a small lad, he had known by sight the succession of painted girls brought into the house by the uncle who had reared him, and why they were brought there, and that the one called "Nancy" was young and desirable and expensive. The old secret, once he had stumbled onto it and put it to use, had gained him control of the store, then financing for buying the saloon, and his marriage to Clarice. As he had told Wendel when he made his showdown move: "Happens that my uncle used to own a whore house in Galveston, Otto. I learned early and I got a good memory for faces. I'm not one to talk when I'm treated right, and I think you and me are going to make a good team out here. You just got no choice, unless you want to pull stakes and leave all this. And wherever you went, there's no guarantee I wouldn't drift along too, is there? Godamighty, the *president* of the Grande Flat Ladies Aid Society! Religion up to her ears. Watchin' them two young virgin daughters like a hawk and hating every man that comes close to 'em. When you two disappeared, Otto, you ran a long ways—but you just didn't run far enough."

50

4.

At the rear table in Ren Blankenship's saloon, Ren and Blackie Toyah sat at a distance from the bar customers. Ren leaned forward on the table while Blackie nervously tossed off whisky.

"What'd you reckon he came back for?" Ren cautiously asked.

"Hell, I don't know. Think he just rode by for a visit with Hinga. Hell, it don't worry *me* none."

"The hell it don't. You *stay* worried."

"Well, if we had our choice whether he ever came back or stayed away, I admit it would be stay away. I don't forget old Clabe Peabody lives for the day he can bang his shotgun at whoever did it. I think the old bastard is crazy and somebody's gonna have to kill him someday."

Ren shifted uncomfortably. "Still seems like a nightmare. Near had it out of my mind till Kelly showed up."

"My gun just went off accidental. I told you two hundred times. But if anything ever happens I get my back to the wall on that, by God *then* it will be Ren Blankenship was in it with me. Don't ever forget that."

Ren's balding head glistened with sweat beads. He had always been a little afraid of Blackie and was conscious that Blackie knew it. "We've got by this long. But I wonder why Saul has come back. Wonder how he got that knife slice? I

51

went down and talked to him a minute but Doc Rice butted in and I didn't get nothing out of him."

"Sonofabitch halfway made to claim he had me arrested. After old Hinga keeled over, Saul was trying to make it he was supposed to carry it out. Then he hit Strawn, so now he's got Bert and Shep down on him, to say nothing of Strawn. You might pass him the word he'd better get out of town while he's in one piece."

"He was always kind of independent."

"Well, I never actually thought much of him. Always with his nose stuck in a goddam book. I bet I told him ten different ways he could have frisked old Hinga out of a little cashbox change there in the office and never got caught. You know how us kids was always broke and how big a quarter looked to us. But he never had the guts."

Blackie glanced toward the door. "Here come Bert and Shep."

The two McQuails walked directly to the rear and kicked up chairs to the table. Without preamble, Bert said to Blackie: "You drunk? You ought to get back home. No use staying around and maybe have that bird jump you again."

"What about the danged bond I'm supposed to make to-morrow?"

"To hell with Kelly!" Bert snapped. "Strawn's dyin' to take care of him, and if he ever crosses me again I'll stomp hell out of him. Ren, haven't you got a little business up front?"

Ren Blankenship trudged away to let them do their private talking.

Bert asked shortly: "What's next with Mendoza?"

"Up to you. Maybe he'll vamoose when he's able to walk."

"I want to keep that greaser in a sweat, and also the Mex drivers that work for him."

"When he gets up from the fix he's in now, maybe he'll be of a mind to sell on your terms and pull out."

Shep McQuail said, "I told Bert if his barn happened to

52

burn and a few wagons with it, maybe that would just about take care of things."

"You two ought to do some of the dirty work," Blackie grunted. "I already stuck my neck out enough."

"Never saw a greaser so damned stubborn," Bert said in irritation. "I made him an offer for the freight business and he turned me down cold. Made me mad. A greaser's got no right to act like a white man."

"Maybe next it ought to be something happening to his daughter." Blackie sloshed over another glass with the whisky bottle. "I wouldn't mind fixin' Alice half as much as fixin' his wagon axle to make that accident."

Shep mentioned that he wouldn't mind that assignment, himself, and Bert laughed loudly and told him he'd better save his ammunition for Connie Wendel. "Hell, I'm healthy," said Shep, grinning modestly.

"Yeah. Well, I'll get on back to the place." Blackie stood and downed a drink for the road. "My wife'll be on the warpath. You take care of that arrest-bond business, Bert."

"We'll take care of it," Bert retorted. "Way we'll take care of it, if that Kelly man wants to play deputy again, I'll shove his damn badge down his throat. Now you keep a tab on the Mendoza outfit, Blackie."

"I just hope to hell none of them greasers try to waylay me," Blackie complained. "Never can tell what they'll do and I don't even have my gun with me."

Shep said, "He ought to have one, just in case."

Bert called Ren, made a request, and in a moment Ren returned with a short-nosed revolver.

Bert passed the gun to Blackie who slipped it into his shirt. Blackie departed through the alley door and mounted the Feeney horse.

The trail west angled downgrade to cross Coyote Creek, and there the lights of town were lost in the back distance. A low slice of moon faintly lighted the wagon road where it dipped into the water trickle among the rocks and branched southwest toward the Mendoza place. The other fork was the route through Buffalo Draw and on to Blackie's sheep range. At the crossing, Blackie, who had found that he was a little drunk, dismounted and set about getting a drink of water. He walked a few unsteady paces to a drinking spot he knew, where the water ran clear before tumbling over the downstream wagon crossing.

Blackie tugged off his hat and tried to balance on his knees and hands, to put his mouth to the cool-running water between two slippery rocks. He tilted off balance on the first try and wet his shirt front. He laughed silently at his own clumsiness, tried again, and noisily pulled in gulps of water. He backed away on his hands and knees, sat up, and reached for his hat.

At that moment he saw movement in the faint light opposite where the wagon tracks sloped down to the crossing. Someone was approaching there, a figure afoot, hurrying, and Blackie stayed motionless until the figure was better outlined.

He moved back toward the crossing and his horse, and met her just as she picked her way across the narrow trickle on the walk rocks.

"Hi there, Alice."

She was across the rocks, and halted now at the edge, trying to make out the man who blocked her path.

"Blackie?"

"Yeah. It's me. You out kinda late, ain't you?"

She paused, then tried to edge aside. Her shawled head was turned up to see him and he could tell there was agitation in her and that she was trying her best to hide it. She was remembering that other time, he thought. The whisky burn coursed high in his blood and began to ignite his brain.

He abruptly made a long reach toward her arm. Nimbly she stepped back. He said, "Kinda lucky, us meeting here again." He felt genial, and made a throaty chuckle. "You outrun me that other time."

54

"I'm in a hurry, Blackie. I have to go to town for something—My father—"

"Aw, let's don't ever be in too *big* a hurry—"

He knew she was frightened, and that she desperately wanted to dodge him when she had the chance and run, and she could run through the trees as fast as a deer. He stretched himself broad and swung out his long arms, ready, and she wasn't going to get past him this time.

She made the try and he dived quickly, blocking her, and closed hard-gripping hands upon her. She fought like a Mexican girl usually fought, silently and with her teeth and her feet when he imprisoned her arms and pawed for her breasts, and the fierceness of their struggle carried them aside into the low-growing brush. Blackie panted with the exertion. He worked one booted foot behind her legs and tripped her. He fell heavily upon her as she struck the ground, hearing the breath knocked out of her by the impact. Whisky and purpose pumped together triumphant as his hands filled with her softness. His weight powered her to helplessness. Her gasping entreaties reverted to Spanish and Blackie laughed thickly and mumbled a Spanish word. He held her with his shoulder and forearm across her chest, and with a free hand he began to tear at her shirt.

She struggled weakly, with all the strength crushed out of her. Something fell from Blackie's shirt, slid across her breast and to the grass. Her right hand touched it, then closed over the stock of a revolver. Blindly, she brought it up and plunged the muzzle into the mass of weight and whisky-heavy force suffocating her, and pulled the trigger again and again.

Saul Kelly went through the routine of closing the building for the night. He secured the front door and blew out the lights, one by one. He walked down the hall and bolted the kitchen door, examined the windows, and extinguished the kitchen lamp.

He returned to the bedroom, removed his gun belt, and

sat for a moment, realizing his tiredness from the day's riding. Grande Flat's day had ended and the outside night had turned silent.

The journey back, he thought, probably had not been worth the trouble. Yet the note had seemed to warrant the trip. It had offered no real clue, almost as if suggesting he was expected to work it out from that point. It could have been a hoax, or a deliberate means of throwing him off some more valid trail.

He had asked his uncle, and Alice Mendoza and Ren and Doc Rice. He could think of no other prospects. If it was intended that the next clue, some secretive word of information, would come to him in due time, then it was the anonymous one's move now. He could only wait a few days to see.

He shifted uncomfortably, not liking the idea of staying longer in Grande Flat. Austin was far east, in another world. Who in Grande Flat could have ever traveled far enough outside to have picked up the story of Arbuckle mountains, Indian Nation, or learned of his Austin location? Yet, in all the months past, no other hint had come to him to match the promise of this one. His long quest had been a series of dead ends. He had made his secret visits away from Austin, empty-handed back again, staying with Dick Hubbard's father, the Governor of Texas, reporting his failures until he was almost ashamed to go back again. And each time, the Governor patiently had said, "Just stay with it, Saul. That's all we can do. It's what Dickie would want."

Dick had been Governor Hubbard's only son and he had died that night in Arbuckle Canyon from a bullet through the heart, when the attackers had struck the two of them in their hidden camp. Dick had been his close friend and travel companion to many places, dating back to the time they first had become acquainted as young boys with the exploration party in Mexico. That night in Arbuckle Canyon he had lost his friend, the money that had been entrusted to them, and almost his own life; and in that disastrous min-

56

ute had realized that someone had followed their trail out of Abilene.

He rolled a smoke, with his mind steadily at work now, thinking back and thinking ahead. Backward, he relived the deep-etched nightmare of the attack, the two sleeping men swarmed by the four, the death bullet for Dick Hubbard, the slash of the knife point down his own face during the struggle, and his fall down the cliff to unconsciousness. There had been a name. *Shawnee*. Sometimes he heard it in his sleep. The thick voice in the dark, calling to one of the others: *Shawnee!*

It later had caused him to visualize an Indian. Yet the attackers had not been Indians. The Cherokees who had rescued him and brought him back to life in their camp had read the sign and were sure of that. By then, the bandits had long since vanished.

Then he thought of the parade of this day's faces as they passed again. His Uncle John, so little changed this morning, and so suddenly gone from the old scene this evening. And Alice Mendoza, Doc Rice and Connie Wendel, the still innocent, delicate china outwardly, and maturely knowing inwardly; and the cagey assured one, Jeb Mott; and Blackie and Ren.

That about called the roll. Nothing linked up. The two McQuails? Lord knew if he ever had encountered big Bert with his mountains of muscles and close-together eyes, he would have remembered him. And the tricky buzzard, Strawn. Anything remembered there? Gunslick was written all over him, but he and Dick Hubbard had seen the Strawn types in many places, the born-mean kind with the small brains and the big guns. Killers, for a while, but dying still young from somebody's gun hand that didn't spook at a reputation.

He crushed out his cigaret, thinking there was nothing to do but sleep in the neat rent-for-$1 room and prepare for a painful day of the funeral procedure. He grinned to himself, because of the irony of the prominent notice he would be roped into as the only kin at the funeral. First and only attention of Grande Flat en masse, he guessed, the Kelly boy had ever received.

He stood and began to unbutton his shirt.

He heard a sound somewhere. Someone knocking.

He carried the lamp and went toward the kitchen, hearing the sound again. A continuous rapping at the back door.

He placed the lamp on the counter. "Yes—who is it?"

"Saul? This is Alice Mendoza."

He unlocked the door and she quickly stepped in, a small tattered sliver off the outside night of blackness and whining wind. He closed the door and stared. Her hair hung in tangles, with a crumpled dead leaf showing ground into her scalp. Her face had a whiteness under the brown skin and a lumpy bruise with blood dots on one cheek. Her dress hung in shapeless disarray with one entire brown shoulder bared by the ripped fabric.

Following down her disheveled and muddy figure, he saw the massive dark stain saturating the front of her bodice. The first probabilities flashed through his mind: a bad fall in the rocks, a runaway horse— Then she whispered, *"Saul!"* and pressed her face into his chest and he knew it was none of these.

He caught her shoulders, seeing only the top of her bowed head. He towered over her, his teeth set hard.

"Who was it?"

"Blackie Toyah."

His mind tried to recede from the impact of that name. He almost gritted out a question, then stopped it behind his teeth. Her appearance was the answer for that.

"Saul— *I killed him.*"

Gently, he held her back and tried to see her face.

"Where?"

"At the creek crossing. I was coming here—he stopped me—he was drunk, and we fought—"

"You know he's dead?"

She nodded.

"You were carrying a gun?"

"A gun fell out of his clothes. I got it and kept pulling the trigger with the gun against him—"

"Does anyone know?"

"Not yet."

She regained her composure and stared up to him with appeal in her eyes.

He carried the lamp and guided her to his room. He checked the window covering again against any escape of the light rays. She sat on the edge of the bed, wiping her eyes, and then tried to pull the torn cloth over her exposed breast.

He felt cold in his veins, thinking of the inevitable. Whatever the circumstance, in this country a Mexican was not permitted to kill a gringo. For that, the Mexican had to run or die. After which, the white men could return their .30-30's to their saddles or recoil their ropes, drink to the success of the chase, and go back to work. A day or two of posse vengeance made an exciting break in the monotony.

After a silence, and with her voice better controlled, she told him.

He listened, and when she had finished he said, "You didn't say why you were coming here."

"We heard tonight of John Hinga's death. My father was very worried. Mr. Hinga knew something of our troubles. These things my father had told him. Your uncle was working on it, trying to find out. Now, tonight, my father wished to know what was next, with Mr. Hinga dead—if you were to stay and be the law, if there was anyone to take his part. We do not know whether to leave the country or try to stay and protect the business he has built."

"So you were coming to see me?"

"Yes. It was decided that I would come and talk for him. He is very agitated, since we heard about Mr. Hinga. My father had asked the sheriff, once, to come up from Kiowa City and help us. But he only said Mr. Hinga would look into it."

"And now it's a hundred times worse."

"I know."

"Even if people didn't think much of Blackie Toyah, there's the border tradition. Your race. You're just on the wrong side of the river. But you know about that."

She said again, "I know."

"So I guess you know all the rest. They will find the signs and know it was a woman. Then the report will spread. Mexican girl, high temper, jealous, long affair with Blackie. Secret meeting at the creek. I can just hear Blackie's wife egging on the mob. The whole Mendoza family would have to run. Even then, the mob fever will burn hot to lynch *some* Mexican, just for a lesson."

"I know. The law on that is written only for the white women."

"Yes. Out here there is no such thing as rape, if the girl is a Mexican."

"Saul—is there *anything* you can do?"

Anything? The word hung mockingly in his mind. Saul Kelly, alone, with gun in hand, braced against all the riffraff, lynch-fevered riders who would assemble in whisky-stoked excitement for vengeance. *White man's been murdered, boys. Let's find the goddam greaser that done it—* A few of the more intelligent townspeople would protest and speak against it. But they would be outnumbered and helpless in the face of custom and superior numbers.

All at once it would turn into righteous obligation. Run the killer down. Blackie's coyote habits would be forgotten, his fine qualities would come to mind and soar to lofty heights with each shot of rye downed along Ren's bar as the posse got itself in top shape for the hunt. *Let's start with that Mendoza gal, men!*

Reluctantly, he recognized the one chance, the only way acceptable to the land, for helping Alice Mendoza.

He said slowly, "I don't know if you'll want to go through with this, but—"

He paused. She said, "Whatever you wish. It has to be in your hands."

60

He gestured to indicate the room, the whole station, himself. "You were here all night. With me."

She nodded her comprehension. "That would be my alibi?"

"Yes. I would confirm that. That is something people would understand and accept. A small incident, of no consequence out here."

"But do you want to be the subject of the gossip? The way the town would talk?"

"The Anglo man never gets blamed in that. It would take care of where you were tonight. Let them hunt for somebody else. It would throw them off the Mendoza track, and I could touch off rumors of the guilty one running for the border."

"But, my father?"

"Not him. Not in bed with a broken leg. Maybe they would try to haze a confession out of the wife of one of your father's wagon drivers. They'll want to chase down *some* Mexican. I would try to cross that bridge when I came to it. Right now I'm only clutching at a way to clear Alice Mendoza and the Mendoza family."

"Are you up to abiding the gossip, Saul? The women of the town would look down on you when they heard—and the very same night your uncle died—"

"Gossip won't hurt me here. I never had much of a standing in Grande Flat, anyway. And I won't be here long."

He lifted the lamp. "We haven't got much time. There are some things that must be done."

He directed her to the adjoining bedroom. He pointed to the bed and tried to smile at her for reassurance. He murmured, "No charge for the room. I guess that would pain Uncle John as much as what I'm going to burn in his big cookstove. I hope your folks won't be worried."

"They will be. They may think that—what everyone else is going to think."

"They'll know better later."

He paused at the door and said, "Get out of your clothes. All of them."

61

Her body was covered by the quilts to her chin when he returned. Her dark troubled eyes worked to him. Seeing her strain, he reached and lightly touched her hair, brushing out the dead leaf fragments. He took her clothing and the lamp, and quietly closed the door. In the kitchen, he built a fire in the big wood range. By midnight, he was feeding in the ripped blouse, the muddy cotton skirt, the underwear, each with its blood-stained reminder of how Blackie had evaded the issue of the stolen Feeney horse but had received the death penalty anyhow in a nocturnal trial on Coyote Creek.

He slid the stove lids back into place to keep the cloth odor out of the kitchen. His own risk, the matter he had not mentioned to Alice, gnawed at him as the mesquite flames ate at her blood-smeared garments. The town would know that Saul Kelly had had his own small trouble, that day, with Blackie Toyah.

With that much of a start, he thought moodily, somebody would be bound to get the smart idea that Blackie had been done in by his old boyhood chum, Saul Kelly. *Hey, men, how about the scar-faced feller that showed up sportin' the six-gun and the law badge, claimin' to be a deputy sheriff?*

The only angle that would bother the saloon lineup of whisky-hot, Winchester-bearing possemen was how Kelly managed to waylay Blackie and still get in a night with that pretty English-speaking Mendoza girl.

That lucky sonofabitch, Ren Blankenship and plenty of others would say.

And the funeral-busy church women would whisper, *Imagine him, taking her right into that building on the very night his uncle died!*

He slipped out the back door, locked it, pocketed the key, and saddled his horse. The night was dark and silent, and he was glad that the pen boy, Jimmie, was sleeping at home and not in the shed. He rode north to the Mexican shacks on the outskirts and rapped on the window of the first house he came to. When a voice answered, he asked in

62

Spanish where Nita, the woman who worked at the Hinga station, lived, and received sleepily spoken directions. He found her house, aroused her, and identified himself, then spoke his request. She did his bidding without question. She thrust the bundle of clothing through the opened door, garments for Alice Mendoza to put on in the morning. He rode back to the station and left the clothing on the back steps, then rode again for the Coyote Creek crossing.

He tied his horse there and went on afoot until he sighted Blackie's body in the low brush. With his vision now adjusted to the night, Kelly sought out the foot tracks the best he could and scraped his boot over the imprints of a woman's shoe. In the few open spots of soft sand about Blackie's corpse, he pressed down his own boot prints. He searched until he saw the starlight reflected on the short-nosed revolver Alice had dropped. With distaste for the job, he fitted the gun into Blackie's cold right hand. If they thought Blackie had emptied his gun at his assailant, so much the better. He remembered that Alice had come to him bareheaded, and that she likely had left home wearing a shawl. He searched until he found it, in the brush, and thankfully stuffed it into his jacket pocket. He could not sight Blackie's horse anywhere and concluded that it had bolted at the sound of the gunshots. Maybe if the horse was intelligent enough, he would drag his reins all the way back to North Arroyo and Feeney, whoever Feeney was.

Then the inspiration struck him. Of course—it was *Feeney* who came down to Grande Flat and waylaid Blackie.

He rode back over the route to the town's outskirts, keeping to the sandy stretches that would sift out his own horse's tracks. He unsaddled in the pen and went to the back door. He entered with the garments borrowed from Nita for Alice to wear in the morning. The faint smell of burnt cloth lingered in the dark kitchen.

Hearing no sounds within Alice's room, he went on to his own. He slept with troubled dreams. In them, he saw both

Uncle John Hinga and Blackie Toyah, so lately departed. The wraith of Uncle John, wearing a deputy's badge, was still trying to make the wraith of Blackie Toyah sign a horse-stealing bond while a nervous, overgrown kid stayed in the background.

5.

Lefty Duncan, an early-riding cowhand from the 97 ranch, was the one who had the honor of discovering Blackie's body in the greasy light just before sunup. It set off for Duncan his most eventful day in years, a degree of prominence in town he had never enjoyed before and won him innumerable treats at the bar from a succession of audiences. Before the Hinga funeral was finished in the afternoon, Duncan had retold his discovery many times, was middling drunk, and had perfected various embellishments including the God's truth that he had seen *with my own eyes* Alice Mendoza standing near naked through an open bedroom door at the stage station. Just her and Saul Kelly there.

Up early and hoping for such a messenger, Kelly was ready. Duncan came in a hurry to tell the part-time deputy, John Hinga. He made his important report to Saul Kelly instead when he learned that Hinga was dead. Kelly saddled and rode back with him to the crossing.

Duncan already had reached a verdict. "Damned greaser done it. Bound to been. High time this country had a good lynchin' to teach them Mexicans a lesson."

"You're probably right," Kelly said soberly. "And whoever he was, he's likely long-gone for the border."

They stood and looked at Blackie's body in the early dawn. Kelly asked Duncan if he would scout the creek bank north to see if he could sight Blackie's horse. This gave him an opportunity to further erase Alice's footprints and signs of the struggle which some sharp-eyed tracker might have picked up later.

The sun was up, coating the creek with a faded-slicker yellow, when Duncan returned, leading the Feeney horse.

"Found him down yonder with his reins snagged."

"He was having trouble over that horse, with a man named Feeney. You suppose Feeney might have trailed him last night and they had a showdown here?"

"Might of been. And again, might not. Beats me how Blackie emptied that gun without downin' somebody. He wasn't that bad a shot. I kinda favor the theory some Mexican jumped him. Blackie was rough on them hombres. They fair despised him."

"Maybe you're right."

"Other hand, could of been Feeney," Duncan debated. His mind willingly went to work, seeing that the substitute deputy needed help. "Feeney didn't get his horse, see, because Blackie emptied that gun at him before Feeney killed him. Maybe Feeney is somewhere mortally wounded. You got your work cut out."

Duncan would be his pipeline to the chase-fevered crowd that would collect. Kelly used him the best he could to plant a tangle of conflicting, but possible, theories. There was one remaining act to play for Duncan's benefit.

When they brought in Blackie's body on the Feeney horse, he invited Duncan into the kitchen, saying he would put on a pot of coffee. The aroma of coffee already boiling on the stove filled the room, Kelly discovered, and felt appreciation for her alertness. Duncan, voluble with his reconstruction of the killing, was unable to conceal furtive curiosity for the tall stranger with the thin scar as Kelly moved about, bringing mugs and the coffee pot. Duncan's flow of talk chopped off as a bedroom door opened in the hallway.

Alice Mendoza stood in full view, straightening the drape of a cotton dress to her body and touching up the night's disarray of her hair.

She waited, showing the proper deference, until Kelly

66

called carelessly, "Come on in, if you want to." Duncan shot a comprehending look to Kelly and back to Alice.

Kelly said, "Thanks for putting the coffee on," in a tone noticeably more tender than ordinary kitchen help would have received. There was something congratulatory as well as hungry in the sly study Duncan worked on Kelly, who was telling Alice about Duncan's find on Coyote Creek. Alice showed the expected surprise, asked the natural questions, and returned to the bedroom carrying a mug of coffee.

Duncan gulped a mouthful of steaming coffee. "Ain't that the Mendoza girl?"

"Uh-huh. We grew up together here. Her mother worked for my uncle."

"Hotamighty!" Duncan made an open grin. Kelly became busy with his coffee but showed a faint responding smirk, as one man to another, to modestly acknowledge Duncan's appreciation for the accomplishment revealed.

"I thought I smelt something like scorched cloth somewhere." Duncan snickered his joke into his coffee mug.

Kelly furnished Duncan an exit by asking him to deliver Blackie's body to the undertaker's house. Duncan was ready to go; the town would be stirring and he had a busy schedule ahead. He almost forgot what he had been coming in for. It was not everyday in Grande Flat that someone discovered the body of a murdered man as well-known as Blackie Toyah, jumped by a greaser or perhaps by a jasper named Feeney from North Arroyo. To say nothing of knowing that a scar-faced stranger, who appeared to be kinda the local law now, had had himself one hell of a big night with the good-looking Mendoza girl.

The church was a hot, squat structure of frame siding nailed by amateur committee carpenters who long ago had dedicated their sweat and busted thumbs to religion under the exhortations of Brother Tatum. Crowded now with warm, moist-talcumed, dressed-up mourners, the room would have browned biscuits even in May, and Kelly was thankful he had most of one hard bench to himself.

The people dabbed at perspiration and fanned with their hymn books. Women located Kelly and whispered behind their hands to their husbands. Those sounds worked in Kelly's ears with Brother Tatum's voice from the pulpit. The drone within merged with the one outside—a windmill's erratic sobbing, grasshoppers clawing the window screens, distant hoofbeats on main street.

When a situation pinpointed him, Kelly knew a way of stepping out of his own skin. From a sideline remoteness he could gauge other people, and himself, critically or approvingly, a way to test the rigging of a ticklish moment. Grande Flat watched him from behind the drone and he watched Grande Flat from the back of his head. He could hear their attention trotting back and forth from the preacher's oratorical streets of gold, Hinga's death, Blackie's murder, some greaser yet to be hanged, and the Kelly man's intimate reunion with Alice Mendoza.

There came a stir within the church and Brother Tatum vocally stumbled a beat. Brought back to the present, Kelly turned and located the late arrival. A ponderous man, unabashed at his lateness, strode the aisle, picked himself a place, and the people on that row slid down to give him ample room. The big gray head with its slab-stone lines locked straight ahead. One glance was enough for Kelly to recognize the stud source of the McQuail features. This would be Brack, the father of Bert and Shep, come to town to pay the respect due a native of John Hinga's prominence.

As the final prayer ended, and before anyone else moved, Brack McQuail made his departure, his duty done. Kelly heard his heavy boots plod the aisle and go out the door.

Kelly filed out with a sea of attention breaking over him, and went toward the buggy he was to occupy with Brother Tatum. He saw the group of town Mexicans standing in the tree grove near the church windows, their way of attending the white man's service. In humble attitudes, the men held their straw sombreros to their stomachs and the women clasped their flowing head shawls to their breasts.

68

Brack McQuail turned his team and buckboard east and whipped away toward McQuail range. During the forming of the procession, a flutter of distraction ran through the church-yard scene when alien sounds floated from across town. A high-pitched yell of alcoholic exuberance was followed by quick-spaced gun shots in a celebrating staccato. Brother Tatum frowned and muttered that some acted like it was the Fourth of July. Women apprehensively glanced at their husbands; men lifted their heads to listen. Some of them pulled out of the cemetery-bound lineup and angled toward town. Others could bury John Hinga as far as they were concerned. An ordeal like Brother Tatum called for a bracing snort and they did not want to miss the gathering of the hard bunch and lynch excitement fanning afire.

After the distant shots, the handful of town Mexicans stayed in an unmoving knot at their place by the church windows, their heads downcast. It was going to be a bad day for some of their people.

Kelly saw that Jeb Mott was one of those who turned toward town afoot, after assisting Clarice and Connie Wendel into the back seat of a surrey. Long-faced Otto Wendel, himself as bleak as a corpse, sat alone in the front seat and handled the lines.

From that distance, Connie Wendel's attention searched for Kelly. Her restrained smile came across to him. Clarice Mott pressured with her elbow, snapping Connie's attention straight ahead. Even the women who had enjoyed a good lashes-wetting in the church were compelled to take their speculative looks. They might have noticed that Señora Mendoza was one of the women among the Mexicans bunched outside the church, but that her daughter, Alice, was not present. And quite understandingly so, in light of the morning's winged news of where she had spent the night.

The word of help needed for a manhunt flamed out over the country.

Men in remote places were glad to quit what they were doing and ride for Grande Flat. In their border doctrine, the finding of an ambushed body of a white brother meant only one thing: a Mexican had done it.

Late-arriving riders tied up at the Texas Bar and joined those already congregated there. They slaked their thirst and asked others for the straight of the killing.

The dusty newcomers heard the details from Lefty Duncan, or secondhand from the next man. They thoughtfully drank their whisky and talked grittily of a way to get started. The problem had a few kinks that had to be thought out.

What Mexican? Where to begin?

The buildup was slow, the start deliberately unhurried. The raw challenge of the impending hunt was interesting to stretch out. For another thing, the situation called for a leader and it took a little time for one to emerge.

Ace Moseley, with two of his Owl Canyon riders, represented the element longest experienced in this, and Moseley was tough and capable in the brush, if not widely admired. For a time, Moseley might have thought he would be the man with the say, but the group began to edge away from Moseley when Shep McQuail entered.

Everybody knew that where Shep went, big-brother Bert wouldn't be far behind, and that Bert was one who had to boss a thing. The McQuail force would outnumber the Owl Canyon bunch, and Moseley saw his prospects for leadership wither. Shep gave Ace a nod, not too much deference in it, and stood beside him midway down the bar. The Owl Canyon *segundo* accepted automatic reduction to a McQuail lieutenant.

Evidently Shep had been in before, and out somewhere. Faces turned questioningly and Shep shook his head.

"He's not back from the funeral yet." He paused for attention. "Just the two Mexican women down there. The cook and the Mendoza girl."

Aside to Ace, he said, "Went to see if that Kelly feller is

inclined to take a hand in this or not. Question is whether we've got a lawman here or if we run it, ourselves."

Ace asked, "Anybody sent for the sheriff?"

"What for? Would take two days."

"I agree. It's a job we can do better ourselves, and a lot quicker."

"Some of us thought we ought to give Kelly the chance. He could either claim to be the law or not."

"Way I heard it," said Ace. "he's not a real deputy. Just happened by and rode along with Hinga."

"I don't think he counts a hoot. Blackie told me and Bert yesterday Kelly was no more of a law than he was."

"Well, we ought to be gettin' at it. Where's Bert?"

"He was over on the north range when we got word and I had to send a man to find him."

"Don't see Strawn, either."

This was a dig on Ace's part; he knew what ailed Strawn. But Shep shrugged and said, "He's nursin' a sore jaw but he don't consider the account closed with Kelly by a long shot. He'll show when he's ready."

Ace did Shep the honors of asking if he had any theories, and the others stood close, listening, calm outside but inwardly tensing up to the job ahead.

"It was a dirty one," Shep grimly commented. "Worst we've had around here in a long time. They say there wasn't a drop of blood left in Blackie."

A fat, bearded man lifted a whisky and said mournfully, "That pore little woman. Widdered in the prime."

Ace cursed. "That's a greaser for you. When they do use a gun or a knife, they go crazy. Situation like this, we got nothing to do but take the law in our own hands, even if we got to work over every Mexican we come to."

"Uh-huh, we give 'em an inch they take a mile," Shep said. "They got to be kept in hand. High time to teach 'em a lesson."

Ace worked a watery red squint around in a critical examination of the help. "I reckon all of you know we got our work cut out. I make a motion the McQuails take charge of this. We've got to organize and work the brush and the Mexican shacks till we pick up sign on the one that did it. The greasers will know. What we've got to do is just pressure one of 'em to speak the name."

He gestured to Ren Blankenship who was lumbering back and forth, helping Joe behind the bar. Ren poured whisky for Ace and Shep, and Ace put down the money for it.

Ren leaned forward, bracing his palms on the counter. Ever since he had heard the news, his mind had been flooded with the imagination of old Clabe Peabody on the warpath of revenge and laying for Blackie. "What if it wasn't a greaser?"

Shep snapped, "What white man would have done it?"

Ren shrugged. Shep demanded, "You think maybe Kelly jumped Blackie, tried to arrest him again?"

"No, I wouldn't say that, Shep."

"We'll wait till Bert gets here. Personally, I think it was one of those Mexicans that work for Mendoza. Blackie had caught 'em on the lease a few times, making to steal a mutton to butcher. Blackie had no love for them and they had no love for Blackie. He made the sonofabitches toe the line. Seems likely one of them was laying for him last night."

Ace said, "All right. We work the country west of Coyote Creek."

"One of them will talk. You bear down on a bunch of greasers with a posse like this and somebody will speak up when they see a few ropes uncoilin'."

"Well, my men are ready to comb brush. Whatever we're goin' to do let's get at it before they get the killer hid out."

Bert McQuail came in then, and attention switched to him. A straggle of other arrivals followed, and the group gave space. Shep told Bert what he had heard from Lefty Duncan while Bert worked on a whisky with deliberate thoughtfulness.

Shep wound it up: "We think the place to start is at the Mendoza shacks, Ace Moseley here and me."

Bert dragged a glance over Ace, not too impressed. But he nodded his agreement and looked wise. "Sure. Any fool would know that. Been hearing a long time about those Mendoza greasers scheming against Blackie. Now, what about that so-called deputy, Kelly? Has he done anything?"

A man chuckled and repeated, "Has he done anything? Hell, the stage building is half off its foundations. Ain't you heard?"

Shep told his brother, "They say Alice Mendoza spent the night with him."

This was Lefty Duncan's cue. He moved toward them, guiding one hand along the counter edge. "Saw 'em myself, Bert. She was in the bedroom this mornin', near naked, God's truth. Seen it with my own eyes."

Bert heard further reports on that and bared his teeth. "Then we're not going to have much help from Mister Kelly."

Shep looked hard at his brother, knowing it was their private purpose to create all the trouble possible for the Mendozas. Bert nodded and tugged up his gun belt. "My idea, we break up in squads and work all the Mex houses to the west. Ren, give me a bottle for my saddlebag."

"I'll pack one, too," Ace said.

Ren began to do a brisk quart business. Jeb Mott, who sat at a table in the background, kept one ear tuned to the cash register, the other to the talk as Bert began to assign men to separate squads and localities to be worked.

As the burial was finished, the cemetery crowd began to scatter and drift for their buggies. As he started for the preacher's buggy, Kelly was confronted by Connie Wendel.

"Saul! Please be careful!"

"Why, Connie?"

"Those men in town. You know them!"

"Yes. You mean anything special?"

Hesitantly, she spoke in a low voice: "Sometimes I can't sleep and I stand at my window and look out at the night, thinking—well, so many things. From my window upstairs

I can see the back of your stage building, the shack where you used to live. Last night I saw the kitchen door open and—I think I saw someone go in, and later you left—"

"It was Jimmie, I imagine. The pen boy."

"Saul, there was a fire built. There was smoke coming out of the chimney at midnight."

His nerves crawled with danger signals. "You must have been dreaming, Connie."

Tautly she replied, "I think I *know*—"

I think you do, too, he thought morosely. Damn, why did she have to pick last night to stargaze?

"Just be careful, Saul. Don't try to cross Bert and Shep."

"Do I hear you right? Shep must be a good man. You plan to marry him."

She spoke a strange confession then, with little-girl candor. "This place is like a trap to me. This land! It's caught Clarice, and I don't want it to catch me! There is so much of the world out beyond—you went away and found it, and I admired you for that."

"You want to break out? Like I did?"

"All my life I have. With the right one, I could—"

Her gaze held steadily as if to tie a hard knot in her meaning. His own narrowed; this was getting delicate. Was she talking *trade*? Then Clarice called "Connie!" and she went, murmuring, "I'll see you later."

Kelly walked to the buggy where Tatum waited. The preacher took up the lines.

"Let me out at the Texas Bar, parson."

"Bad bunch collecting down there."

"I know."

Alighting in the street, Kelly saw the horses tied in the mesquites and the men talking on the plank walk. The group spread for his passing and some of them followed him inside.

He stopped at the near end of the counter. Ren Blankenship came forward with a bottle and said, "This is on the house. My best."

"Thanks. I can use it after Brother Tatum."

Lefty Duncan's words cut through the silence: "That's him!"

Bert, Shep, and Ace moved toward him, establishing that end of the bar as a headquarters, and the crowd pressed around them.

"Well, let's get at it, Kelly," said Bert without preamble. "We've got men here and we're ready to start smokin' out the Mex that did it. Where's your big badge?"

His tone struck Kelly as more than a bully's challenge; there was a mocking taunt, a hidden something to come. Kelly worked a glance from the McQuails and Ace over the hard and weathered faces beyond.

He nodded. "So I see. What did you have in mind, Bert?"

"We figure it had to be a Mex to pull an ambush like that on Blackie. We're agreed we'll work over the ones that live west of Coyote Creek, to start."

Bracing an elbow to the counter, Kelly invested a full tally on the gathering. The sorriest scum in a place, he thought, were always the first to want to mob a black or brown man. He faced back to Bert.

"There're Mexicans all over the country. They all look alike."

"Maybe so. But it's a way to start. One'll be enough. What one knows all of 'em know."

So this bunch had made up their minds; they wanted the excitement of the manhunt. Even those who might befriend a Mexican, who daily worked with Mexicans, would fever to pull a hanging rope once the mob excitement got out of control. And no one man could stop them. He could only attempt to tangle their doubts.

"There's another possibility, McQuail. Something my uncle mentioned to me. Seems there's an old codger around with some kind of crazy notion about Blackie."

Bert snapped, "Who?"

"Clabe Peabody."

Kelly shot a look at Ren Blankenship who noticeably jerked. Little sweat beads dotted Ren's scalp.

Someone said, "Peabody never carries anything around with him but a shotgun."

Lefty Duncan braced himself behind Ace Moseley. "Tell 'em about Feeney."

Kelly complied. "Besides Peabody, there's Feeney. Blackie was in trouble over that horse. Any chance Feeney might have waylaid him?"

"Hell, I don't know!" Bert said in irritation. "You might have got the itch to do it yourself."

"I wouldn't have gone to that extreme, just over serving a warrant."

"Feeney lives 'way up at North Arroyo," Ace objected.

Minds about worked on the possibilities. A few cool heads, Kelly was thinking, was the most he could hope for. Enough to dilute the fever a little, a few to object when a drunk showoff wanted to ride down the first Mexican they came to.

"We could talk up theories all day and never get anywhere," Bert said doggedly. Men watched expectantly, remembering that the stranger had challenged the McQuails yesterday. A quiet fell, and Kelly knew in his bones that Bert was going to say the obvious.

"Kelly, maybe the first thing we'd better get settled is whether you're a deputy sheriff or not. If you're not, we don't need you atall—you can get on back to your dish of *chile con carne.*"

Men grinned; some of them chuckled. Good-naturedly, no offense meant, and Kelly understood. They granted one another the privilege of that color of opportunity in a land devoid of larger selection.

But Bert intended to push it farther. He squared off and raised his voice. "You're not actually a law, Kelly. We all know that. I think maybe you're just a lit-tle bit too thick with the Mendozas to do us any good on what we got to do. This ain't a job for a greaser-lover."

The land's cheapest insult hung there, rancid like the bar smell, saturating the room. Kelly felt his face burn; when he reddened, the scar line would whiten. The group waited, to

76

see if the new man wanted to make anything of it, against the McQuails, and did not blame him when he didn't.

He said, "I'm sending for the sheriff. He can get here by tomorrow night."

Bert grunted, "We'll attend to things, scar-face," and led Shep and Ace in what became a general drift to the street.

Jeb Mott came to Kelly from a silent half-dozen men who lingered in the background, most of them town-dressed. Mott said briskly, "Let's talk a deal on that Hinga property. Sooner we close, sooner you can get out. Might be a good thing for you to leave before Strawn comes back. I'm trying to do you a favor."

Kelly stiffened and stared down at Mott. Then he controlled himself and tried to cover his distaste. Mott would be the type who knew everything. So he murmured, "Yeah, we'll talk about it later."

He shouldered past him. As he pushed through the door to the sidewalk, he heard Mott say to Ren Blankenship: "You know what? Right there's the guy that killed Blackie. Bet you money."

"It don't make no difference," Ren replied glumly. "What that bunch wants is to shoot a greaser."

6.

Doc Rice alighted from his buggy as Kelly emerged to the walk. Clutching his peeled bag, Doc headed directly for the saloon steps and Bert McQuail.

"What's the plan, Bert?" Doc's voice was controlled but raspy.

"We're going to run down the greaser that killed Blackie."

"Now look here, Bert—there's no sense in this mob chousing out there and hazing the Mendozas."

"Sense in doing whatever it takes to find the one that did it."

"Now wait a minute," Doc raised his voice. Kelly pushed through to stand beside him. Otto Wendel, with Jonesy the blacksmith and two other town men, came across the street. Up and down the walk heads craned from doorways. Doc looked from Kelly to Wendel and the others, and then at the men flanking Bert.

"We had a little talk at Otto's store, some of us. There's a few here that're opposed to this lynch-mob business. We want Blackie's killer run down, same as you. But we want some law and order in it. There is absolutely no purpose to be served by this bunch going out there and roughin' up some innocent Mexican just because he can't speak enough English to alibi himself. We're asking you boys to break this up."

He was the doctor, he had known the ailments, private

and public, of most of them, a spokesman entitled to a degree of respect. But Kelly doubted that just Doc Rice and the uneasy business men would be enough to stop them. Bert McQuail had bunched himself up into a thick storm to fight for his leadership. He drawled contemptuously, "What did *you* have in mind, Doc?"

"We agreed, some of us, to ask Saul Kelly to be our deputy sheriff and let him take charge till we can get the sheriff to come up here from Kiowa City. This is a thing that needs the regular law ahold of it."

Kelly heard the rumble of protest. Bert heard it, too, and became sure of his ground. He peeled down a mouth corner and winked at the men siding him. "Well, ain't that just fine, Doc. *We* agreed—now who in hell is *we?* This bunch here didn't vote, did they?"

Otto Wendel said, "Kelly is Hinga's nephew. Hinga made him a deputy, way I understand it. The town has got to have a law of some kind and he's the logical one."

"The way you understand it!" Bert snapped. "Christ, does bein' a man's nephew make him a law?"

Doc whirled to Kelly, opened his mouth, closed it, with words cut off. Kelly read his question. He was asking, would Kelly identify himself? Kelly shook his head, knowing it would make no difference. They would pay no more heed to a foreign federal lawman than to a local deputy sheriff. Probably less; their resentment to interference by an outsider would only fan the fires of violence higher.

Ace Moseley spat to the street and shifted his tobacco knot. "So we stand here and run off at the mouth while the murderer gets clean away. Next thing you know some damned bandit will waylay another one of us. Might even be one of our wimmin. Country wouldn't be fit for white people to live in. We let them greasers get out of hand, and we're ruined. I've seen it all my life." The ancient sentiment of the land came out of Ace by rote and sounded like Gospel.

"Yeah, we got a job to do, Doc," Bert said,, taking attention back from Ace. He faced about. "Any of you too squeamish to help, stay here. The rest, let's get moving."

Not all of them had the stomach for it. A few hung back, pretending various attentions to horses or saddlebags or a last-minute errand. Kelly counted twenty men who rode, with Bert, Shep, and Ace leading the way toward Coyote Creek.

The town men stood silent in the street as if embarrassed by their impotence. Doc Rice scowled at Kelly. "You going to send somebody to bring the sheriff?"

"Already have, Doc. This morning."

Kelly hurried to the station building. He found Alice and Nita in the kitchen. Both their dark faces raised to him, strained and questioning. He spoke to Nita: "Is the pen boy out there? Tell him to saddle my horse."

Nita departed and Alice came to him, a slight figure too small for the borrowed dress, and caught both his arms. "Saul, what are they going to do?"

"Make a little trouble, maybe."

"Did you send for the sheriff?"

"No. Decided not to. Doc Rice just asked me that—I lied to him."

"Is it because—?"

He nodded. "Sheriff might be smart. He just might run down the right answer. I don't want to chance that."

"Are you going out there?"

"Soon as I can get out of these church clothes." He smiled for reassurance he did not feel. He went into his room and changed to his range clothes and a canvas jacket, and came out strapping on his gun. Nita had returned, and he beckoned Alice out of earshot.

"You stay here, now. Right in the station. If the bunch brings anybody in tonight, they'll headquarter down at Minnow's wagonyard. They'll get liquored up. No matter who you hear they've got, don't go down there."

Fiercely, she shook her head. "If they hurt my people— I will tell everyone how it was—"

She did not resemble the shy girl he remembered. In that moment he saw more panther than fawn in her dark, livid eyes. He said, "The truth in this wouldn't help. They would twist it to suit their own purpose. It would tie in the Mendoza name directly. So far, that bunch is only casting around in the dark."

The panther look gave way to a woman's tears. "Why does it have to be a *Mexican* they must butcher—?"

"You know the answer to that as well as me. They don't have a white man prospect." He grasped both her shoulders. "Tell me straight—is it the McQuails who have been badgerin' your family? Trying to buy the freighting business?"

"Yes. For a year they have made trouble."

"Brack, the old man—or just the boys?"

"The boys I think. Bert, mostly."

"I'm going now. I'll do what I can. There's a thing or two I'll gamble with, if necessary. Listen, now. There might be—there just might be a caller, come to pay her sympathy or from curiosity or something—"

He hesitated and she asked anxiously, "Who?"

"Connie Wendel," he said uncomfortably. "I don't quite know what to make of her—but you be careful, especially if she starts asking questions."

"But Connie is my friend. We both taught during the school term. Does she suspicion—?"

"Just a caution," he said evasively. "Maybe she won't come. Idea is, you be careful, no matter who comes nosing around."

He left her standing alone in the front room and went to the pen gate where Jimmie waited with his saddled horse. Jimmie was puffed from the tension that gripped the town. "Where's the lynchin' goin' to be, Mr. Kelly?"

"Not decided yet. You look after things."

Kelly put his horse in a gallop for Coyote Creek crossing.

From across the street and a block down, Jeb Mott watched through a dusty windowglass and saw him go. For a while he looked at the Hinga building and pens, and then decided that he would go down and make a closer inspection as the prospective new owner. As he left the store, he saw with surprise that Connie hurried along the sidewalk on

81

the opposite side. He waited, and watched his sister-in-law go on to the next block and turn in at the station entrance.

Word could mysteriously fly on invisible wings through the distant stretches of the brush land, and by now it had the momentum of nearly a full day to travel. Word went out to white men to rally as hunters; to the Mexicans that their breed would be the hunted. In the remote line camps and lonely adobes, wherever a Mexican worked singly or amid a drove of relatives, old fears throbbed like rot in a wound. Brown-skinned aliens kept inside their shelters, as if safety lay in pretending invisibility.

The Mendoza place appeared deserted when Bert McQuail's detachment from the posse walked their horses into the long shadows of the clearing. Bert had assigned this target to himself, bringing Shep and four others. He studied the shaded house and the scene downgrade where the pens and some of the freight wagons stood. Along a ravine beyond that were the adobes that housed the Mendoza workers and the workers' families and their assorted kin who seasonally came in irregular migrations. Nowhere was human movement in view.

"We'll work the main house first," Bert directed. "Shep, you and Billy and Ponch ride down and keep a watch on those shacks. Nab anything that tries to run."

Each man had pulled his Winchester from its saddle boot. Bert and two others crossed the yard afoot. Bert directed one to circle and cover the rear of the house. At the porch Bert called: "Mendoza! Hey, inside! Show yourself—pronto!"

When they heard no response, Bert thumbed back the hammer and fired his rifle from the hip. The slug smashed the upper edge of a window pane. Glass sprinkled to the porch floor.

"That ought to bring somebody out."

The older man, Jeeter, said hoarsely, "I wouldn't have done that, Bert."

Señora Mendoza emerged from the shadowed hallway.

82

When she saw the pair with their rifles ready she momentarily drew back.

"Why you do that, Señor McQuail?"

"Why don't you answer, woman, when somebody calls? Who's in there?"

"What do you want?"

"You know what we want. Who you got hid out around here?"

"None hid out."

"Where's Mendoza?"

"In bed. He has the broken leg—"

"Yeah, yeah, we know all about Mendoza's leg. Who else you hidin'?"

"There is no one, señor."

"Stand aside, woman."

"You have no right—"

"We got plenty of right. This is a legal posse. This is the law—"

"My husband—he is sick—"

"He's liable to be sicker. Move aside. We're taking a look."

Bert jerked his chin at Jeeter and thrust Señora Mendoza aside in the doorway. Jeeter reluctantly followed and grumbled, "I don't go for roughin' up a man with a broke leg."

The other man, Brisco, a McQuail range hand, came in at the rear and met them in the dogtrot corridor. Through an open door they saw Mendoza stretched on a bed. His legs were uncovered and one of them was stiffly sheathed in Doc Rice's splint and wrappings from ankle to thigh.

"Look in the other rooms," Bert ordered over his shoulder. He advanced to the bed with his rifle ready. He slapped a heavy hand over the bed and groped under the pillow.

"No gun? Keep your hands in sight. Now which one of your outfit waylaid Blackie Toyah last night?"

Mendoza replied in careful Enlish: "I've been expecting you. That shot through my window—that is not going to be forgotten."

"Making threats again, huh? Think I remember you made threats against Blackie."

"I don't know who killed Blackie."

"You're a liar."

Brisco came back, reporting there was no one else in the house.

Bert grinned down at the gray-stubbled face in the gloom. "Mendoza, where's your daughter? How come she's not here?"

Mendoza stared back without blinking. His wife stood at the foot of the bed with her head downcast. Bert cradled his rifle. "You probably know about that as well as everybody else in Grande Flat. In case you don't, though, I can tell you something that ought to make you feel real good. She spent the night with the Kelly man at the stage station. Now ain't that a fine way for a nice educated Mexican school teacher to act?" The man and woman stayed silent.

Bert said, "Mendoza, I made you a pretty good offer so you could sell this outfit and vamoose. I think you've hemmed-and-hawed about it just a lit-tle too long, but you still got a chance. Now you know this country don't like for a Mexican to set himself up like you've done. You're going to hub all kind of trouble if you stick around here. You be thinking it over but you better think pretty fast. You're not fooling us one bit—you know who murdered Blackie Toyah. Not a Mex in this country does something without you know about it. Now I'll not drag a man out of bed with a busted leg, unless I've got to. We'll work on the rest of your bunch and one of them had better spill it. If they don't, I'll be back to see you."

Bert lumbered out with Jeeter and Brisco following. "Now we ride down to the shacks and see what we can turn up," Bert said. He delayed to pull the whisky bottle from his saddlebag, took a long swallow, and passed it to his hired rider, Brisco. Brisco gulped and passed it on to Jeeter who was looking thoughtful. Jeeter had a small place somewhere on the stage road south and had ridden with a couple of posses in the past, Bert remembered. Jeeter had his slug and inquired flatly: "You been badgerin' Mendoza to sell to you, Bert?"

"That's private business, Jeeter."

Bert and Brisco mounted and spurred their horses for the workers' adobes. Jeeter elected to walk, leading his horse and not hurrying.

Approaching Coyote Creek crossing, Kelly fell in with two latecomers who were riding to find the main posse. Like all the others, they had their holster guns, saddle rifles, bedrolls, and bags stuffed with supplies. They quietly looked over the stranger and accepted him as bent on the same mission. One of them, a husky, square-chinned graying man, said briefly, "I'm Elrod, foreman for Oglesby," and waited, his glance holding direct, so Kelly spoke his own name, adding, "John Hinga's nephew." The other man had ridden ahead on the trail, and pulled up at the crossing where a rider waited. He said he was posted by Bert to direct latecomers. "Bert and Shep and some of 'em went for the Mendoza place," he reported. "Ace Moseley and a detachment are swinging south to comb those Mex nesters below Crosscut Trail, and another bunch is circlin' north of Buffalo Draw. I reckon you can ride to join any one of them you want to."

Kelly asked, "What if we don't flush anything before dark?"

"Bert said everybody was to rendy-voo back in town at the wagonyard for the night. Minnow's barbecuin' a calf and Jeb Mott's supplyin' the beer."

Elrod looked about and remarked, "This where it happened, was it?"

"Blackie was right over there." Kelly pointed. "He was in a little trouble over a horse belonging to a man named Feeney, up at North Arroyo."

"I know Feeney," Elrod said shortly. "He's not the kind that would ambush anybody but he sure wouldn't hesitate to face a man in the open. If he said his horse was stolen, I'd be inclined to believe him."

85

Kelly took a second look at Elrod and liked what he saw. Then Kelly said he would ride for the Mendoza place, and Elrod and the other rider said they would too. The younger remarked, "That's where the excitement will be, like as not."

They came into the Mendoza clearing just as the sun nicked the rocky bald line of the Chisos Hills, coating the mesquites in a liverish orange twilight. Voices sounded indistinctly toward the ravine. In that instant, they sighted someone making a jogging run in the trees, toward a pole stock pen. They turned in that direction, sensing that action of some kind centered at the pen. As they came upslope, Bert McQuail and three others were grouped afoot, listening to Billy Jebson.

"Shep got him one," Billy was reporting. "The greaser spotted us and busted out of that last shack yonder. Me and Bert choused him all through the brush. Shep caught him in the open and threw a rope on him. The hombre got dragged a little, fightin' it, but Shep's leadin' him in."

Bert spoke with satisfaction: "We'll just see what the old boy was doing all that running about." His glance took in the newcomers; he said "Howdy, Elrod," and his attention stopped on Kelly. "Usually, when one takes off for the brush he's got a good reason. Ain't that right, Mister Kelly?"

"Would seem so. But not for ambushing Blackie Toyah. The man who did that wouldn't be waiting here all day in a shack for a posse to show up." Kelly kept the tail of his eye on Elrod as he replied to Bert. Elrod squinted and watched Bert, as if expecting an answer to that. Bert muttered, "Well, we'll see about that." The whisky bottle passed from Bert to Billy to Brisco.

Shep, wearing a grin of pride, walked his horse out of the mesquites. His rope stretched back from the saddlehorn, pulling a thin-chested young Mexican with a dandy's sideburns and hairline mustache. The captive's pants hung torn and dirt-stained. His loose shirt was ripped and thorn scratches showed on his forearms and face.

"Here's us something, boys!" Shep called out in studied

nonchalance. He played in his catch. The Mexican stumbled forward. His eyes swam in white depths of terror. He mumbled, "No spik *Inglés.*"

The group looked him over with interest. Bert remarked, "They never do speak English, do they? Not when you need to get something out of them. Any of you know this one?"

Nobody knew the cringing man still held by the taut pull of Shep's rope. Bert asked in labored Spanish: "What's your name?"

"Vicente Elisondo, señor."

Bert said, "Somebody ask him what he's doing here and where he's from and all the rest of it—"

"Maybe I can talk to him," Kelly said. Without waiting for Bert's approval he addressed the Mexican. After a time, Kelly turned to the others. "He's a relative of one of the Mendoza families, visiting the place. He spooked and ran because this bunch plain scared hell out of him. He implied he was in the cabin with a woman he wasn't supposed to be with."

Bert bleakly studied the prisoner. "The truth ain't in 'em. A couple of you go in the shack and talk to the woman. Search it for a gun that might have done in Blackie. Kelly, ask him how he got that dried red mud on his feet."

Kelly asked it. Vicente, sweating, replied and began gesturing but Shep jerked on the rope and the captive fell.

"He says something about hiding out in the brush," Kelly translated. "I gather he was afraid the husband would show up."

"Sounds reasonable to me," Elrod said shortly.

Bert disagreed. "Yeah, and that mud could have come off Coyote Creek, too. Whole thing sounds thin—Hey, you, Vicente—you savvy Blackie Toyah?"

The Mexican was trying to ease the knot of Shep's noose. He shook his head. *"No sabe* Blackie Toyah, *señor."*

"Who brought you up here to kill him? Mendoza?"

Vicente pointed toward the distant adobe. *"Prima mia—"*

"The woman is his cousin," Kelly said.

"Oh, his cousin imported him for the job, eh? Vicente—

your cousin told you where to go waylay a white man your relative didn't like? You shoot 'em—" Bert cocked finger and thumb, enacting a revolver blast. The Mexican talked excitedly in Spanish, shaking his head.

"He's trying to say he came to see a woman cousin," Kelly broke in. "I think it's plain he was just in the wrong house at the wrong time. He's edgy because he got caught in a bad situation and he knows all the Mexicans are edgy, too, over what happened to Blackie. I suggest we turn him loose and look for a better prospect."

"Now, wait just a minute. There are just too danged many people around here that were having fun last night with Mexican gals." Bert waited, grinning. Elrod looked puzzled. Kelly was off his horse and walking toward Bert. Then Brisco and Ponch came up, hurrying from their search. Brisco held up a small revolver.

"Found this hid under the mattress. Woman in there, scared white. She won't admit nothing."

Bert examined the load and squinted in the barrel. "Been reloaded. Barrel's dirty. Just the size that could have ventilated Blackie." He walked to Vicente, towering over him. "This yours, hombre?"

Vicente shook his head. Bert swung his open right hand and slapped the Mexican on one side of the face and then the other, and kept it up, the slaps smacking right and left until Vicente went to his knees.

Kelly reached for Bert and swung him around with a hard twist to his heavy shoulder. Bert pulled back with the pleased gleam of fight in his eyes. Kelly's hand whipped and his sixgun levelled on Bert's middle. "Not the time for fists, Bert. Right now, this gun says you lay off Vicente."

Bert opened his mouth. Then he froze. Kelly had been forced to turn his back on Shep. He heard the step close behind him, heard Elrod's raised voice say, "No you don't—" and saw the stretched rope go slack. He tried to turn, dodging, but Shep already was swinging with his fisted Colt. The solid steel smashed the side of his skull and the ground exploded under his feet. He found himself in the dirt, trying to say *Shep, I owe you for that* when the hazy circle of boots melted in fog, first gray to his vision, then in blackness everywhere.

Consciousness returned slowly, and with it a burst of head pain. He opened his eyes, saw that he was in a room, on a bed; saw the lighted lamp on a table, the Mexican woman beside the bed and Elrod in a chair against the wall. Kelly tried to sit up, and managed it after the first spell of dizziness.

"Take it easy," Elrod said. "You got a hard lick."

The woman had been holding a wet cloth to his head. She stepped back. Elrod said, "She's the cousin."

Kelly managed to sit on the edge of the bed. "How long have I been out?"

"Not long. The others rode for town. I stayed around— some Mexicans came out and helped me tote you in here."

"Thanks for staying, Elrod. When they rode off—did they take Vicente?"

"Yeah. Bert said it would be a heap more comfortable adjournin' court to the wagonyard than out here. He sent out men to bring in Ace Moseley and the others. You feel like riding?"

"I feel like it." Kelly stood, finding his legs wobbly, but achieved a balance. The woman retreated to the shadows in the corner.

"Got a little out of her," Elrod said, standing. "Told her Vicente might stretch a rope if she didn't tell the truth. So she admitted that he was here with her last night. All night."

Elrod extended his gun and Kelly returned it to his holster. The woman murmured in Spanish, "The bleeding has stopped, but you have a bad bump."

Kelly fingered the knot above his ear. Elrod said shortly, "Those McQuails are fast to rile up." Then he asked curiously, "You ever had a run-in with 'em before?"

Kelly took his hat from a chair, expressed his thanks to the Mexican woman, and tried his legs for a few paces before answering. "I don't know, Elrod. I just might have. A long time ago. Something strange, maybe familiar, went over me when I was going down. Or maybe I dreamed it." Elrod asked no further questions. Kelly saw no need to add that, as he had sunk into unconsciousness, his whirling brain seemed to hear a voice call in the blackness: *Shawnee! Shawnee!*

7.

On most nights, this time of Spring, the town turned comfortably quiet in its lonely isolation. The long benediction of a soft May twilight finally would fade out and the drape of a vast night would come to tuck in the miles of despondent greasewood and thorny mesquites. Lamps turned shaded windowpanes into reminders of habitation when the houses themselves dissolved from view. After night closed down, sounds traveled far in the thin clear air. There weren't many; nothing much astir to make sounds. Windmills working; the crickets and the dogs; but these were a fixed part of the night silence. Barn doors closing where people went about after-supper chores. Often, the far-off singing and chords of a guitar from a back yard in the Mexican settlement. And mixed with that, until late, musical laughter. Grande Flat, if the night was not Saturday, had the world to itself alone, in a corner of a county a day's journey wide, and it was a waste of fancy to vision a world outside any different. Later, but too soon after Spring, would come the sapping heat and drought of summer, with the universe baking and giving off a hot flannel-rag smell. Red dust would blow. Tempers of men, longhorns, irritable rattlesnakes, and coyotes bold for water, would shorten, sometimes flare out in violence. Old feuds might boil up, into Saturday fist fights in the street or saloon alley; occasionally, a killing. These would furnish the town a summer subject to gnaw on clear through the winter.

This was the Grande Flat as remembered by Saul Kelly.

But May-evening peacefulness flew apart, this Tuesday night.

Word spread to supper tables behind the blobs of window light: the posse had captured a Mexican, the killer of Blackie Toyah. They had him tied up at Si Minnow's wagonyard. Some said he had confessed. Others heard that the posse had yet to work a confession out of him. For what that suggested, some approved, some cautiously dissented. The strong-stomached talked hard and spat in the street from where they braced along the awning posts. The meek listened with inner excitement, and hung about, not wanting to miss anything. Only a few of the select, known to be qualified, were admitted to the working force gathered out of sight behind Minnow's fences. The two McQuail men and Ace Moseley were in charge down there, and it was reported to be a legal posse, because the posse leaders themselves had so proclaimed it. That was all it took.

And like another small tremor following the town's big shake, came along another report. John Hinga's nephew— *you remember the Kelly boy?*—had been involved with his second run-in with the McQuails. Kelly, they said, was wanting to take up for the Mexicans, was siding the Mendozas. And no wonder.

Mrs. Henrietta Forbes, visiting the house of neighbors, took the opportunity to say that she herself had seen Saul Kelly when he rode into town only yesterday. She parlayed this small distinction, of a sort, into comment that she had utterly no idea at the time that he might have come back on account of Alice Mendoza. This made interesting conversation. Then Mrs. Forbes speculated aloud that Señora Mendoza had worked at the stage station for years, until Mendoza got his freighting business paying off. Not that she had ever heard anything out-of-the-way about John Hinga and Señora Mendoza. But it was an interesting thought, now. It was only a spur-of-the-moment comment, but Mrs. Forbes went home feeling that she had contributed something.

Kelly rode to the stage pens from the back way. He heard the later-than-usual sounds of movement over on the street. He could see horses tied at the rail at Curly's Cafe and farther down at the Texas Bar. Then he noticed that Alice, or perhaps Nita, had lamps burning behind every room in the building, from front to back. In the past, this would have meant that the small bedrooms Uncle John offered to transients had been rented for the night.

Just before he dismounted, Kelly noticed another light, not so cheerful.

The glow of open flames and wood sparks spiraled into the night at Minnow's wagonyard, visible above the dark bulk of the stable buildings. He visualized the posse there, passing the bottles around a bonfire in Minnow's corral. And the terror of the Mexican whose fate was being debated. They would drink and discuss, loudly for Vicente's ears, a dozen crude methods of making him talk. It was the way to work on a stubborn Mexican—make him go nearly stark crazy with wondering what the bunch were going to do behind the privacy of Minnow's tall board fences. All over Texas, the regular law often did the same, out of sight in the jails; the free-lance possemen just copied the methods with certain embellishments.

As he unsaddled, Kelly thought morosely if only Vicente, yesterday's dandy moth, had not been drawn back today to the flame. Then, angry at the idea, and at himself, he refuted it. Vicente had his rights, if they could be called that, and owed an accounting, if any, to fate and circumstance unrelated to Blackie Toyah. Nor to that drunk collection of avengers whose small minds had to have it that the whole white country was on test, endangered by the brown.

As he fed his horse in the darkness, it came to him that Uncle John was someone to miss. This was the night and the posse's bonfire glow marked the hour when he felt any depth of regard for Uncle John. Affection might not have been one of Uncle John's strong traits. But in those other years the boy had understood that his uncle was a hard-headed moral symbol, curtly no-fooling beneath a thin surface affability and righteously mean enough to cause the troublesome to think twice.

Remembering that, he turned without special purpose to the adobe shed, pulled open the crookedly-hanging door, and put a match to the lampwick. The wall shadows sprang into place, so familiar to him they seemed to deserve speaking to. He sat on the edge of Jimmie's cot, once his own, and idly took the anonymous note from his wallet. He studied again the pencil-printed words. A man's hand, he had decided, not feminine, though this could not be told with certainty. The clues there were meager. Words were spelled correctly, the lettering practiced, not crude. The Laredo postmark had meant nothing. But someone had known to address him by name properly, at the U.S. Deputy Marshal's Office, Austin. He let his mind work with the knowledge that the McQuails had made a market drive to Kansas last year and the year before, as Ren Blankenship had revealed. That was a little to go on. But who was an Indian somebody that might be called Shawnee? And outfits all over the country, as well as the McQuails, had made market drives to Kansas.

To get at the job, he thought, he must cautiously work out more information on the McQuails. And it would have to be done in great innocence, with the utmost disguise possible. Further talk should be attempted with Ren Blankenship, Doc Rice, even Jeb Mott; and perhaps Otto Wendel, though he was a close-mouthed one; and with Connie Wendel, who should know small details about Shep, her intended, if anyone did. He shifted uneasily, remembering Connie's implied knowledge of the hour when someone —Alice?—had entered the stage building's rear door last night.

And as he thought of Connie, he heard light footsteps outside. He hastened to replace the note in his wallet, the wallet to his pocket, and to stand with his gun hand ready.

94

The sagging door squeaked open. The shaft of light re-vealed Connie, materialized from his thoughts.

She blinked against the lamp glow, cautiously edged in-side, and pulled the door nearly closed behind her.

"I always wanted to see inside this room," she said shyly.

He smiled at her across the cramped space. "In those days you would have been very welcome, but I would have been too astonished to say so."

"And now?"

"Well, it's still a surprise."

He motioned to the cot, sat on the edge of it himself, and she settled primly to the edge at the other end, smoothing her dress over her knees. "I was just leaving the station," she said in a self-consciously lowered voice. "I saw the light back here and guessed it would be you. Jimmie had re-ported sometime ago that the chores were finished and that he was going down where the big excitement was."

This prospect seemed less likely than any of the others, but he would use the opportunity while it was available. "Connie, did you write a note to me recently?"

She replied, as Alice had, "No, Saul. I never knew what became of you. To me you were a vague remembrance. A little girl's memory of an older boy she never really knew."

Carelessly, he asked, "You visited Alice?"

"Yes. I thought she would be anxious. There is so much tension in town tonight."

"Anxious about what, Connie?" He studied her closely, trying to find where the truth was in that blandness.

"Why, all those men going out to her father's place. I had been to see Alice earlier, and left. Then I heard that her parents were not harmed. I saw Shep on the street after the posse came in and he told me. So I came back to reas-sure Alice because she would want to know. She had been very concerned."

"You saw Shep?" He touched the throbbing bruise on the side of his head away from her.

"Yes. After they brought the Mexican in. He told me

that the Mendozas weren't bothered, that the posse had found the Mexican who killed Blackie."

"Shep's and Bert's version. The Mexican spent the night in a Mendoza shack with a woman not his wife."

She murmured thinly, "Such an outbreak of the romantic we're having around here!"

"Happens all over the world, Connie."

"I suppose so. Was bound to seep out in Grande Flat."

"Connie, can you help get it over to Bert and Shep that they've got the wrong man? I'm going down there and try to convince them. I have another witness to what the woman said—a man named Elrod. He's convinced Vicente is innocent. We need all the help we can get. Your influence would count."

Her glance turned troubled, raised to him, guiltily fled to the floor. "I don't have any influence, Saul. Shep had been drinking. He boasted about roping the Mexican. And that he had knocked you down when you tried to take up for the man." She hesitated, then continued in a shy tone. "This was on the sidewalk and two or three men were with Shep. And it was there and then I knew beyond doubt I never wanted anything to do with Shep McQuail the rest of my life. I told him so. There was a small scene. Very embarrassing. The other men grinning—"

He considered that, and visualized the proud, drunk Shep getting his romance spattered on the street like a dropped melon, with his henchmen witnessing the upheaval. Dryly he said, "Then I guess one good result has come out of a mean situation."

"It was bound to happen," she said with husky emotion. "At first I liked Shep, a little. You know the choice is not very great out here. But after they came back from the trail drive two years ago—something about them, Bert and Shep—somehow they changed. Shep was different."

"In what way?" *And keep talking, little one. Let it pour right out!*

"I don't know what it was. Some invisible something.

96

Something—distrustful. And that horrible man Strawn who came back with them from the first drive. Their good friend, they said."

"Their good friend is a dead-brained gunslick, if I know the earmarks. I've seen a few."

"I have a little respect for Brack, their father. He's hard, and he let Bert and Shep run wild. But he's honest. He can't abide Strawn, either."

She stopped and he prompted, "When did they come back from Abilene, that drive two years ago? What month, I mean."

"Oh, I don't remember. September, I think."

"With plenty of money, I take it. From the herd sale."

"Oh, yes. Shep was proud. He told me they had brought three thousand dollars in cash to Brack and had another five thousand coming by bank draft."

"Three thousand? Brack's money, I presume?"

"Of course. He had sent the boys north in charge of the drive and to collect the cash payment."

"He trusted his boys, then? Not afraid they would gamble away his money in Kansas?"

"I should say not! Brack would have skinned them alive if they hadn't been able to account for every cent. But why would all this interest you?"

"No reason at all. Maybe it's just because you mentioned you broke up with Shep, and because anything about you, Connie, might be interesting to me."

She flashed a quick examination to his expression, probing for sincerity. She laced her fingers in her lap and smiled briefly, glancing over the room. "When we were children I always wanted to see inside this room, where you lived. Mama would have died at the idea."

"You were here a few times. In my thoughts." It suddenly came to him that this was so.

"The whole place could use a woman's touch. Are you going to sell to Jeb?"

"We're going to talk about it. Connie, what did you and Alice discuss?"

"I just wanted to pay a friendly call. We have a little in common, you know, both being school teachers. And when I came back the second time it was just to tell her that the Mendozas were not harmed." She added casually, "And the oddest thing—Alice had on a dress that originally was my mother's."

"Mrs. Wendel's dress?"

"Yes. I noticed it was too large for Alice, then I recognized it. We give old discarded clothes to some of the town Mexicans. You know, we all do that. This dress had been given to Nita, your uncle's housekeeper. And there it was on Alice."

"They pass them around, I guess."

"It's the first time I ever saw Alice in somebody's cast-offs. She's very good at making her own clothes." Now she gazed directly at him. "Alice is a pretty girl. That lovely complexion and fine eyes! Very appealing in anybody's cast-off clothes. It's too bad she's Mexican."

He reached across the space and caught her hand, not certain himself whether he was playing a game because she might be dangerous, or whether he had always wanted to know the touch of her and had never dreamed it would be possible. "You're a pretty girl yourself, Connie. I've never forgotten."

With his fingers tightening on her hand, she slightly inclined her body toward him, and in the same moment he heard the sound at the door.

Alice Mendoza stood poised in the opening. He saw the catch in her breath, the surprise, her lips part, then close. Kelly drew his hand back and Connie straightened in a guilty movement.

"Pardon the interruption. I saw the light—" Alice spoke in thin aloofness.

"No interruption," Connie said calmly. "I've been asking Saul what can be done to help that poor man they have down at the wagonyard."

Alice stayed poised in the readiness of a wild bird about to fly. "I was to tell you, Saul—Dr. Rice and Mr. Elrod and some others are going down there with *guns!* They mean to prevent those men from mistreating Vicente Elisondo."

"I'll go." He started to say more, but Alice whirled and vanished into the dark corral. She was hurrying out the main gate when Kelly and Connie left the room. They walked to the gate and Connie's hand brushed his. Her fingers lightly closed. They walked with her head almost brushing his shoulder.

They continued across the station side yard to the street, not saying anything until they paused there. He murmured, "Thank you, Connie. You don't mind going home alone?"

"I'm used to that. That big empty house—. Mama's on a visit in Del Rio, a delegate to a church convention down there. So I guess it is another night by myself."

"Dreaming at the window?"

She tilted her head sideways for a veiled glance up at him. "Maybe." Then, with a shake of her head: "But not likely tonight. Not with all the trouble in town. I probably will want the window closed tight and my head under the covers."

"You don't feel bad about—what happened between you and Shep?"

"I don't feel bad about it at all. I feel like I came to my senses just in time, to cut the only tie that would have kept me in Grande Flat. I feel *free*, Saul."

Alice stood in the center of the station's front room, waiting for him, her feet braced apart. The loose dress draped her small hips and outlined her boyish thighs, hanging too long for her height and giving her the look of a child playing dress-up. Her face was dust-streaked. Flinty purpose struck sparks in her wide dark eyes. She held an opened bottle and a wadded cloth in her small brown hands.

"Come here!" she ordered.

He advanced warily. "What're you—?"

"Be quiet! Bend lower, I can't reach up to the moon."

She upended the bottle to the rag. The fiery smell staggered him. The burn hit like a smithy's red-hot tongs when she pressed the soaked cloth to the blood-dappled blue bruise over his ear.

He gritted his teeth. "What in the name of God you trying to do—?"

"You're hurt. I doctor you—"

"It wasn't hurting till now—"

"Some people would be so pretty-kitty as to never think a man might get the gangrene—"

"Horse linament! I know that smell! You trying to kill me?"

"It is very good. It works on horses. Also mules."

She swabbed a new application and the burn watered his eyes.

"Damn it, do you have to set me afire!" Her swabbing was none too gentle.

She stepped back, her head tilted high as if to assess the damage. "Now. That's the best I can do. Dr. Rice might do better, but who knows how to find him in a time like this?"

"It burns like hell on the loose."

"Never mind. You were already burning, I think. It is so warm in that little shed room. Now, maybe I have cooled you."

He stared down at her, aware of a scratchy edge of fight in her voice.

"You might have been killed!" she said accusingly. "When I heard, I was afraid. I walked the floor. I sent Nita to try to find the doctor. Shep McQuail had left you for dead for all I knew. Then there you were in the shed room—" Her chin quivered.

"It wasn't much," he mumbled. "The damned linament is worse than the lick."

"*Si*. So I found out it wasn't much."

Her puzzling antagonism abruptly crumbled. Her stiff shoulders went slack. The little belligerent chin came down and she whirled away. She hurried around the counter, put the bottle on a shelf, caught up a dust cloth and began

100

wiping at layers of red dust. He followed over, guiltily. "You've got cobwebs in your hair, dirt on your face, and Lord knows what on your mind. What are you doing?"

"Housecleaning! This long day! I had to do *something!* When a woman can't bear the wait, when her heart is a hurting lump, my mother says she should tear into the kitchen, bake a cake she never tried before, start a sewing, clean the house. Anything. Heaven knows this place needed it. Then tonight we had the big rush."

"What kind of rush?"

"She—Connie Wendel—came back. Jeb Mott came when she was here the first time. Smoking his big cigar and prowling all over. Then room customers. I became very busy. All the rooms—they had to be tidied. They are rented for the night. You will have to sleep in the shed and I will stay the night with Nita. She is no help here, out front. But I remembered everything to do—the register, the keys, the rate. From so long watching Mr. Hinga."

He leaned against the office counter. She had turned her back and now attacked the dusty shelves with the cloth.

"Your family is all right, Alice. Before I left out there, I went by to see them."

"I heard. It is now Vicente Elisondo who is in trouble. He has been inviting it—that one! But not trouble like this. Mr. Elrod told me."

"Elrod was the one who stayed and helped me when I was knocked out. Later, he rode on in when I went over to see Ferd and Maria."

She paused and turned anxiously. "I hope you told them I am—that it is all right."

"Enough that they understand, I think. Where did you see Elrod?"

"Here. He is one who came for a room tonight."

"Elrod's stopping here? Who else?"

"The register." She pointed. "Trade got brisk and all at once I found myself running a hotel. This is a big night in Grande Flat."

He looked at the yellowed open page of the room book, saw a couple of scrawled signatures above Elrod's, then whistled.

"Mack Feeney, North Arroyo! So he showed up! What's Feeney like?"

"Like—like a walking clump of dried-out prickly pear. I heard him say to Elrod he came looking for Blackie Toyah and a horse. Then he heard about—Blackie." She faltered at the name. "Then he said that the country would survive that loss but he still wanted his horse, anyhow."

"Any of them in the rooms now?"

"Everyone has gone down to the saloon or to the wagon-yard. The town men want you down there and I am hurting inside me with fear for you to go."

"Now, about Connie. And dammit, I didn't invite her to the shed." He stopped and wondered how he had got on the defensive. "What did she have to say?"

"Just talk. The first time. That Jeb Mott was tromping all over the place. Once she said—" Alice averted her glance and lowered her voice. "She said something like, 'lucky girl.' She smiled and I just smiled back. Perhaps I blushed. If not, I know I am blushing now."

"She didn't probe around, ask a lot of questions? About last night? Or that dress?"

"It was hard to tell what she was after. She noticed this dress. She talked about—*you*. The next time, when she came back, it was to say she heard my people were not hurt. And she told me she had a breakup with Shep McQuail."

"So did I," he said tiredly. "And I think a bigger one is due."

He saw the small tremble in her lips. "Saul, I am not afraid of Connie. She is kind to me, she is good. I will not say anything against Connie Wendel. She would be a good —a good *wife* for someone—she deserves better than this town. She is not the proud one like Clarice Mott."

She turned her back and listlessly swiped at the office table. "Will you want some supper?"

102

"I won't take time. Maybe I will eat barbecued mutton with the jolly posse down at Minnow's."

He walked out. Her call came faintly, *"Please, Saul—!"* He kept his course to the dark earth sidewalk and then south on a broomweed-bordered path, striking across two empty blocks to the wagonyard where the bonfire sparks drifted skyward. His long legs covered the distance in measured strides, not slow, not fast. The back route took him into darkness well away from Curly's Cafe and the Texas Bar, places where knots of men gathered with mob violence smelling the main-street air like rotted steer carcass. The dark route to trouble; not his own doing, not relished, nothing to do with his only purpose here, the one big purpose he had lived for. Blackie Toyah was nothing, no more than a dirty taste from the past. Vicente Elisondo, just something from across the border he'd never heard of until this insane day. Too much; too many things, were roping him in. Not a damn one of them worth killing a man for or being killed about. None but the one *big* thing. That, and only that, was what he had meant to save his gun for. *Then why in hell do I mess with the little problems of Grande Flat?*

Out of the darkness, his mind's eye caught sight of the cold Indian eyes of John Hinga, the sparse grin, not really friendly, hidden behind Uncle John's mustache droop. No, damn it—it wasn't that. He hadn't owed Uncle John a thing. He had given him a decent burial, sweated through that eternity of a church service, had obligingly pinned on that damned deputy star for the ride to Blackie Toyah's.

Well, he was nearly there. He would go on to meet the rubber-kneed town men, try to talk them out of violence, and see if the trouble might not just fizzle out of its own accord. One Mexican cut up a little—hell, even one Mexican hanged—wouldn't be a loss long remembered. Wouldn't be the first time out here.

He came off the broomweed path to the rutty side road and made out the knot of men grouped a distance back from Minnow's wagonyard main gate. The long row of stable buildings cut off view of the open space inside, but faint flickering light from the corral bonfire touched and streaked the faces that turned to watch his approach.

Doc Rice was first to detach from the group and advance a step or two.

"They chased me out," he grumbled. "They got a hangnoose over that Mexican's neck."

8.

They were a hesitant dozen or so, all the village could muster to go to the brink and not quite up to going all the way over it. Prudence would tell a peaceable man he was wise to stay out of it, not to get crossways with the McQuail bunch. They stood in the sandy road back from Minnow's gate like boys without the price of circus tickets and looked at Saul Kelly.

Jonesy cursed as a strong introduction to a weak pronouncement. "We can't even get in there to reason with 'em. Maybe you can."

"Why do you think I can?"

"Why, you're Hinga's nephew," the blacksmith replied. "Kinda the deputy." He meant that settled everything and stared in genuine puzzlement when Kelly drawled, "He didn't will me Vicente Elisondo."

Another man said, "John Hinga would've been in there reasonin' with them, gettin' that Mexican turned loose. There's some that would have listened to him."

"I'm not John Hinga. I'm not a deputy sheriff. I'm a foreigner. I happened in town on other business—" His mouth dried out on dust, the words gummed in his throat, bitter to taste. Damn them—they had reached back across years of nothing, dragged a strong-backed kid out of the horse pens, stuck a star on him by the simple assumption of inheritance. Before, they had barely known he existed ex-

105

cept as a fuzzy-faced wraith with a pitchfork in a cloud of hay and alley dust.

A man on the back fringes cleared his throat and made a couple of false tries before he got God into it. Kelly sought out the shadowy shape. It was Brother Tatum. "Kelly, there are some—mind you it is not *me* pretending to pronounce judgment—" The preacher fumbled at his text, found it. "The women in the church—good people—well, some think it was—er, unbecoming, the way you took that young woman right into John Hinga's house—him barely gone to meet his Maker."

"Thank you, Brother Tatum. Thank you for this kind opportunity to go in there and redeem myself."

Doc Rice craned up at him. "That gun lick Shep gave you hurt you much? Maybe I'd better get you in a light and look at it."

"It's all right. I've been doctored."

"Concussion would leave you sort of groggy. You feel dizzy?"

"Not in that department, Doc. What's the situation in court?" He gestured toward the high board gate.

"They ran me out. Me and Jonesy and a couple of others."

"What about the Mexican? What have they done to him now?"

"Had a noose around his neck and the rope over a tree limb. Just part of the hazing while they get likkered up. Only thing, before long some drunk cowboy may want to pull on the rope a little. A little too much."

Kelly started for the gate in the high wall. The group spread, then hesitantly closed behind him. A voice he recognized as Elrod's said, "Most everybody here has got a gun. We'll back your play, whatever it is."

"I'd rather you stayed back. If you crowd in like making a battle out of it, that's what it will turn into and somebody will get hurt."

"They won't let you in," Jonesy warned. "Got a guard on the gate."

106

Kelly paused. "Where's Si Minnow?"

"He's in there. They just moved in on Si—he can't do anything about it."

Kelly shook the gate and found it locked. Distant fire glow faintly showed the man who appeared at the crack and growled, "You-all go away. We'll call you if we need you."

"Open the gate!" Kelly ordered.

"Who're you?"

"The deputy sheriff."

"Didn't know we had one." The guard chuckled.

"You're finding out now."

"Not 'less Bert or Ace say so. They've gone to the saloon. You wait till they come back."

Kelly shifted and pressed his left shoulder against the boards. He levelled his Colt. The explosion rocked the planking and the lock shattered. He threw his weight against the boards and the heavy gate swung back, downing the man inside. The guard struggled for his gun and Kelly struck down with his boot. He tugged the gun out and stepped back, passing it on to Jonesy who had followed. "You hold this one outside."

He slowly walked around the corner of the stable row. The fire centered the scene, showing the men squatted on their heels or braced on the hay bales beyond a wooden water trough. The shot had turned the delegation into a momentary freeze of movement. The colors of the still picture began to smear with motion as the fire glow identified the intruder.

Shep McQuail jerked into movement when the collection of eyes flicked from Kelly to him. He gladly accepted the appointment and collected his muscles to meet it. His sense of the spotlight churned faster than his mind worked and all he got out on the spur of the moment was, "Oh. The amateur deputy. We don't need you."

"Where's Bert? I want the head man."

"It's none of your business. Now you vamoose."

Shep paused on the fringe of the group, to the right of the water trough. Kelly angled to the left of it, out to the edge of the light. He stopped by the lone dejected figure of Vicente Elisondo. The Mexican stood under the dark spread of a pin oak tree, slumped as if tired from long standing. His wrists were tied behind his back. A rope trailed up from his neck and over a limb, the loose end dangling behind him.

"We'll just take this rope off before somebody gets reckless. This is not the one we want."

Shep called, "Goddamit, Kelly, you drag out of here!" and began an advance that had to circle the long trough between them. Kelly saw the others shuffle in uncertainty; it was written in their expressions that they were interested in the prospect of a McQuail challenged again by the stranger.

From the far edge of the light, at the stable corner, came Elrod's raised voice: "Kelly's right. Like I told you fellows, we did some more checkin' and I'm satisfied this hombre is the wrong man."

Any but the most bullheaded would hear Elrod with respect for what he had to say. He was known to them, and that, with perhaps their own secret doubts, may have stayed their hands. All at once Shep hesitated, as if sensing he was standing alone. Kelly pulled his knife, keeping hurry out of his movements. He slashed the rope binding Vicente's wrists. He began to work at the knot at the back of his neck, seeing Shep advancing again. He murmured in Vicente's ear: "There will be much *tumulto*—watch your chance and fade over that fence in the dark and keep going."

The attention of twenty-odd possemen prodded Shep, perhaps against his will. There was Elrod backing Kelly's play, and now a knot of town men had paused at the stable corner where they had part-way followed. *He will have to keep coming*, Kelly thought, without appetite for it. He closed the knife and pocketed it. Shep, with his giant size and reputation and narrow between the eyes, was already too far started to back down. The complete silence was enough to say it was a bad night for Shep: with Bert gone,

108

with the men knowing he had been jilted by Connie Wendel, with the newcomer wearing the purple knot where Shep had gun-slapped him from the back, and the newcomer now carefully placing his sixgun on a hay bale as he watched Shep approach. The posse settled in hot and alcoholic appreciation.

Shep waited no longer. As Kelly lifted the hangnoose up and over the Mexican's head, Shep came in a rush of speed and power. He arrived with the force of a mad stallion, both arms swinging. Kelly dodged late, miscalculating the explosive speed of the big man's attack. A fist like a balled steel chain smashed the side of his head, almost in the bullseye of the raw bruise already there. The ferocity of Shep's attack, the unholy pain of the tender wound resliced, sent him reeling. Red streaks crackled in his skull, and he was on the ground.

Struggling to get up from his sprawl, he had no protection when Shep steadied, took aim, and kicked him under the ribs. Kelly's muscles quit and he lay facedown in the dust, twitching, breathing the powdery manure. He clawed with his hands, fighting to get his face up. He twisted his neck. He had to find Shep and searched for him in the crazy spinning night of fire and darkness.

When he found him, Shep had his gun out, his arm upraised, aiming to exactly plant the swing. *Shep's one that loves to pistol-whip,* Kelly thought in detachment, watching trancelike as Shep got set. Shep's legs were spread and Kelly swam into them, clutching, entangling—as much to have something to hold on to as for any other reason, and Shep's swing missed completely. The arms wrapping his knees sprawled him off balance to a jolting sit, the gun flew out of his grasp, spinning halfway across the pen.

Kelly ducked his head and held on, knowing this big man was all rock and hard to hurt. Shep kicked wildly, trying to get free of the octopus entangling his legs. Kelly lost his grip, but he had a second to scramble back, to fight up to his knees, then shakily to his feet. Shep struggled

109

erect, too; he steadied, spat aside, fisted dirt out of one eye and took a deep gulp of breath. With his chin hooked down to his collar bone, he nailed a practiced evaluation upon his foe and then came again to finish him.

Kelly sidestepped, covered, weaved, blocked the fists the best he could and retreated. He fought back at the dozen bared-teeth spinning faces of Shep. He parried, eluded, gave ground. Dreamily he fought the big man who seemed to be everywhere. His retreat carried him, fighting, to the edge of the water trough.

In all this time, he confusedly believed he had not hit that oncoming wild giant a single decent lick. Yet, his arm bones ached from something. He retreated and worked his dead arms in a blurred pumping, and something must have connected. Shep grunted loudly and stumbled. In that precious second of respite, Kelly grasped the edge of the water trough to steady himself and backed around its end. He slapped his right hand into the water and threw a cupped palm of it into his face, smearing its good cold wetness all over. Then Shep was back at him, viciously fast, and they collided. Kelly heard the crack of bone against bone and the great gush of lungs and smelled an outpouring of whisky foam. Surprised, he peered through hurt and rolling sweat to see Shep drooped, his guard down, dazedly wagging his ·head and his chin throwing off blood. Kelly backed three steps around the corner of the water trough, then Shep collected and powered after him, but he was throwing his fists wildly. His head was down and his body was bent for a dumb bull rush. Kelly dully remembered what to do about that, and he twisted to his right with instinctive footwork and straightened Shep's head with a left uppercut starting low, from below his left hip. Shep jerked like a man who had butted into a door edge in the dark and appeared to have lost sight of Kelly.

Kelly hit him in the stomach. Something sounded like a cow splash and Shep shuddered, clutching at Kelly, then hanging on to him, burying his face into Kelly's shoulder.

Shep's dead weight drove Kelly backward on numb legs, and the back of his knees struck the edge of the water trough.

Shep clung on with his blind embrace and Kelly felt himself falling backward over the trough. He threw his hands out to brace his fall and twisted in a full-length flip to dislodge Shep and get from under him. Shep slowly floated forward and Kelly hit him twice in the mouth and jaw with his freed right hand as Shep tilted headfirst over the trough side.

Shep feebly caught at the worn, slick edges of wood and Kelly raised his boot and crushed the heel of it grinding into Shep's clutching left fingers. Shep gave out a high moan as his grip came loose. The moan was cut off by a splash and a gurgle. Kelly had Shep's left arm bent and locked high behind his shoulder blades, and his right hand spread and shoving down on the long-haired crown of Shep's head. Now Kelly poured down all the strength he had. Shep's head went down and out of sight, and water soaked halfway up Kelly's forearm. Bubbles roiled the scummy water. Shep kicked convulsively and flailed with his free right hand, his shoulders, with anything a drowning man could move, and this turned into a dying-perch flopping until Kelly felt the movements begin to tone down.

There was no man moved to come to Shep's aid. Kelly tried to see them through the salty sweat clouding his vision, even as he watched Shep's headless shoulders. The weakening flames showed a collection of erect men strained and staring in studious attention at a drowning in two feet of water. Kelly relaxed his right hand a little. Shep fought his head up and took air with a crying gulp. Kelly smacked down on Shep's head again and waggled the locked arm higher, and Shep's face went under. A crusted bullfrog croaked and soared from the far end of the trough into the darkness and every spectator jumped. Shep kicked and floundered. The water boiled in a hundred noisy bubbles, and then all the kick went out of Shep.

Kelly caught him by the back of his collar and pulled him out limp and Shep began to draw rattling, body-shaking breaths. Kelly held him until he would stay drooped on his own feet, running water out his nose, spitting water, rattling his lungs. Kelly adjusted him and hit him with a measured right uppercut exactly to the underside of Shep's jaw. He hit with the hard heel of his palm, to save knuckle bones, and the jolting connection jarred him to the shoulder. Shep sat down, almost gracefully, and then folded over on his left side beside the trough and lay as still as a sack of oats.

Kelly peered through the blur, trying to see the others. The one he remembered as Billy Jebson slid his gun nearly out of its holster, then back. Kelly saw them looking beyond him. He shifted and saw the town men at the corner, in the far edge of the light. They had guns in their hands, a curious assortment of big and little hand guns.

Kelly moved to the trough and washed his face with bleeding fingers. He noticed that the place where Vicente had stood under the tree was now empty.

That was all that Kelly had time to see and remember.

Commotion ran through the night behind him. He looked back and noticed the town men giving way. Bert McQuail stormed through, with Ace Moseley close behind him. Bert stalked ahead on a crest of whisky smell and unbridled anger and Kelly dully thought *He's even bigger than Shep.* Bert squinted from side to side, at the town men, at the others, then at Shep on the ground and to Kelly turning back from the trough.

Not up to it, Bert. Not right now.

He didn't think he could lift his arms again.

It didn't matter. Bert was a vast rock slide tearing apart his guard. The first woodchopper blow sent Kelly reeling. The earth flew up to smash him. Far off in blackness he thought he saw a business-like Colt in Elrod's hand, and heard Elrod calling, "Now that'll be all for tonight, Bert."

112

Grande Flat coal oil burned late; some of the lamps, all night.

Reports of what had happened at Minnow's corral seeped into the houses like red grit through the planking and eventually out to the sweeps and folds of the country. Saul Kelly had whipped Shep McQuail, nearly drowned him in Minnow's water trough. Bert had come and knocked out Kelly who had been carried away unconscious. A few town men—brave ones, everyone agreed—had drawn guns on the posse. The wild bunch had chosen not to trade bullets with another set of white men, just over a fight. Ace Moseley had had a disagreement with Bert over a scheme to retaliate against the Mendoza Mexicans and had pulled his Owl Canyon men out of the hunt. The ambush-murder of Blackie Toyah was unsolved, back where it started. Hints laced the reports that perhaps the McQuails were making some kind of personal vendetta out of it, against Mendoza. Two men, Elrod and Jeeter, reliable ones, were rumored to have said so; some claimed that was why Ace Moseley had pulled out.

When a shaft of early sunlight sliced through a window, Kelly became aware of its glare and opened his eyes. He knew that this was the shed room, that hands had tugged and pulled at him at intervals all night, arousing him to foggy consciousness between stretches of drugged sleep. At a sound on the floor he twisted to see Jimmie, dressed except for his boots, sleepily sit up on a pallet.

"You feelin' better, Mister Kelly?"

Kelly mumbled, "I don't know yet." He was afraid if he moved the pain would come back. "What was going on here last night?"

"We waked you ever' hour, like Doc Rice said to. Me and Alice Mendoza. Doc said white pill one hour, green one the next, cold water bandage and ointment in between. He wrote it out." Jimmie went over to the table and looked at the doctor's note of instructions and the watch lying beside it. "Time for the white pill again."

He brought a pill and a glass of water. "Doc said it was important to rouse you ever' hour. He didn't want you plumb out all night. Account of that head lick."

Kelly worked up to his elbow, took the pill, swallowed water, and groaned. Then he sat up all the way and waited until the room steadied.

Jimmie watched with special interest. Kelly said, "Thanks for looking after me."

"You whipped Shep McQuail," the boy said with respect. He added, "This is sorta interestin' work for me. Sorta like doctorin'. I'm good with animals, and I've helped Doc before. Different people call me in when they's somebody to be sat up with."

Jimmie began to work on his boots. "The last man that was sick on that cot, name was Taggert. He fell off a windmill. He died. Right there."

"Encouraging." Kelly steadied himself on the bed edge and tried his legs.

Jimmie frowned. "Doc said stay in bed till he looked at you—Yessir, Taggert died. I helped Doc with him from start to finish."

He had no interest in what Jimmie was saying. He tried his arms, his leg muscles, found that he could stand. Jimmie watched with professional interest. "You sure talked loco when we would wake you for medicine," he said. "Reminded me of how Taggert was before he died. He talked out of his head, too. The last few hours he would say the same thing over and over, you know, like a dyin' man does, fightin' at death a-comin'. Taggert would say 'Arbuckle Canyon, Arbuckle Canyon' and sometimes I would have to hold him down. He died right there on that cot.

Kelly shook his head to clear it and eased back to the cot.

"He said *what?*"

" 'Arbuckle Canyon'—"

Kelly felt a sweat break out. He stared so fiercely at Jimmie that the boy drew back. "Who was Taggert?"

"He worked around the country, different jobs. Fell off a

114

windmill, on his head. Didn't live but two days. Now I got to get at the feedin' and waterin'."

Jimmie left. Kelly gingerly worked on his clothes and his gun, which someone had restored to his holster. He looked down at his old cot—the very place Taggert had talked out of his head and died. Then he made the long limping walk to the station kitchen in search of coffee.

9.

Main street turned warm by 9 o'clock Wednesday when the creosoted wind licked in with heat off the greasewood. Unshaven men with whisky-puffed features came out of the wagonyard in relays, made their way to Curly's for breakfast, and trooped back in the middle of the street to the wagonyard again. One of them was Bert McQuail, unspeaking, ponderously thoughtful. Another was Shep, lumpy-faced, pale, and limping.

At 10 o'clock the watchful street observed another rider come in on the east road. He trotted his horse the length of the street and only Jeb Mott spoke to him as he passed. Jeb gestured and called, "Strawn." The rider, decorated by a red-streaked bruise from chin to socket, flicked an indifferent response and rode on to the wagonyard.

Mott stood on the edge of the porch at the City Mercantile, apart from a group occupying the whittled-up bench along the wall. They saw the gate at Minnow's open for Strawn and close behind him.

Otto Wendel said uncomfortably, "Seems the sheriff would have got here by now."

Elrod remarked, "Maybe he didn't want to ride it. Maybe he's coming on the evenin' stage tomorrow."

"Could be he don't want no part of it," Jonesy suggested. "What if he's not comin' at all?"

Mott said, "Yeah. And maybe Kelly never sent for him.

On account Kelly got smart and tried to arrest Blackie, himself."

Mott looked at the bench lineup through a puff of smoke. "That big play you-all made last night—you bucked the best bunch of customers this town's got. You get the town all crossways with the cattle outfits and Grande Flat will dry up and blow away. I don't know as that was very smart."

Doc Rice stared at Mott. "You would have let them hang that Mexican, maybe maim Kelly?"

"Listen, Doc—they're going to get 'em a Mexican anyhow. Everybody knows that Mendoza camp is a hangout for half the bandits on the border. Maybe it would be a good thing for the country to run the Mendozas out and have some white outfit operating that freighting business. One Mexican bunch like that right in our backyard draws all the criminals off the Rio Grande like flies to sorghum."

It was an old-debated subject. The talk died. The group silently studied the street toward Minnow's. After a time, they saw the procession emerge.

A string of riders. Bert McQuail in the lead. Strawn, Billy Jebson, Brisco. Ten or twelve in all. A ragged parade, coming north on the street.

Doc Rice commented, "Mostly McQuail men. Now where do you think they're headed?"

The riders turned west on the cross street, and the question was answered.

Elrod murmured, "Going toward Coyote Creek. I guess the Mendozas are not out of the woods yet."

"Shep's not with 'em," Doc noted. "Hear he's in the saloon applying whisky to his pride."

Jeb Mott tossed his cigar to the dirt and started a diagonal crossing toward the Texas Bar. Wendel held his sour stare on Mott's back for a moment and then trudged toward the rear of the store.

Doc Rice asked, "You going out there, Elrod?"

The range foreman considered, then shook his head. "No-o-o. I've about had all of this business I want. I thought it was a bonafide manhunt for a killer. I'm damned if I know what it is, now." He stood and reset his hat. "I've got a hundred sections of range to look after and work enough to last me till winter." He stalked away.

Doc Rice lifted his bag. "I've got to go see how Kelly is."

Jonesy stood. "Well, we made our little sashay last night. About as far as this town wants to go, or can. My livin' is runnin' that blacksmith shop and I run it or don't eat."

The group broke up. Clarice Mott and Connie Wendel came upon the porch from the walk on the east side. Jeb Mott glanced back from a distance. Clarice wigwagged to him, but Mott made a curt gesture and continued toward the saloon. Clarice voiced a word of impatience. She turned into the store doorway and noticed Connie had paused.

"Aren't you coming in to see Papa?"

"I'll see him later."

Clarice lowered her voice. "I think he's looking bad. I don't think Mama should have gone off—"

"She'll be back on the stage tomorrow."

Clarice said accusingly: "That trouble between you and Shep! That will hurt Papa. You have hurt us all, Connie. That scene right on the street!"

"The family will survive the disgrace."

In sudden suspicion, Clarice demanded, "Where do you think you're going now?"

"To the Hinga station."

"Why *there?* That Kelly man—the Mexican girl—"

"I think the Mexican girl is going to need some sympathy before long, with the posse on its way back to the Mendoza place."

She started north on the walk. Clarice called sharply, "Connie!" but her sister kept going in brisk and independent strides. Wendel came from the back of the store. Clarice said with exasperation, "I don't know what's got into Connie!—Papa, don't you want to go home and rest? I'll keep the store. I don't think you look well."

118

Otto said hoarsely, "I feel all right. Was just being up so late last night." He hesitated. "I'm riding down to Hunt Goodman's place this evening. I'll spend the night with Hunt and meet the stage when it comes through there tomorrow and ride back with your Mama. Mention it to Jeb."

"Why don't you mention it to Jeb, Papa?"

"Probably won't see him. He'll be helping at the saloon all day. They're having a rush of trade."

"Papa, is there some kind of—well, strain, between you and Jeb?"

"Why, nothing that I know of," Wendel said shortly. "Must be your imagination."

Doc Rice found Kelly in the front room of the stage building, drinking coffee at the domino table. Rice frowned and put down his bag. Kelly touched his Colt and asked, "How did I get this back?"

"Elrod picked it up when they were carrying you out. You ought to be in bed. We may be fighting a concussion."

"You sure fought it. People shaking me awake every five minutes all night."

"Wasn't five minutes. Was once an hour. Now let me look at that head."

Doc removed the bandage and made an examination. "Better shape than I thought."

"Better than the last man you bedded down in the shed room. Taggert?"

The doctor squinted. "Oh. Jimmie must have told you. Yep, you're a danged sight better off than Taggert was. He died on me."

"Doc, thanks for what you and the others did last night."

"By gad, that little bunch showed some spunk, didn't they?" Doc said proudly. His tone changed to a morose grumble as he stared out the window. "Everybody brought whatever weapon they had and they faced up to that bunch. Far as they could. Only so far people can go out here. Nobody wants to get classified as a Mexican-lover."

"Yeah. Healthier to be a McQuail-lover, I guess."

"Kelly, this is the last pimple on the face of Texas. People just do the best they can because it's a hell of a long way back to conventional law and order and civilized courts."

"You and the others bucked the mighty McQuails last night. Otherwise I probably wouldn't be alive."

"We were a white bunch and they were a white bunch," Doc tried to explain. "Nobody was going to do any killing, either way. Now if it had been Vicente down in the dirt instead of you, maybe Bert McQuail would have kicked his brains out and nobody would have pulled a trigger. That posse down there—they're kinda the real backbone of the country, one way you look at it. No other stripe could hang on out in this desolation. It takes a mean streak in a man to match a mean country—the longhorns and the brush and the odds. Some of them are the scummiest bonepickers in creation, high-handed as hell when it comes to greasers. The sorriest drifters show up out here. They're white men and they got to prove something so they prove it on the greasers. They'll tuck a pint of whisky in their gut and get up and ride that old Texas Alamo business and that old San Jacinto business like halfwit kids on a stickhorse—and all that happened forty years before some of them were born. They were spawned hearing that one Anglo is worth twenty niggers and ten Mexicans and that's about all some of those bastards *ever* had to be proud about in their whole life."

It was a long speech for Doc and he ended out of wind. Kelly said, "I remember, growing up out here. I remember how it was."

Doc scowled. "It's a country where a little man gets to walk big. Even the best-intentioned. It was no picnic to live in when the Comanches and the Mexicans were contesting the whites every step. But who was to cull out the no-goods? Country's not much, but even the meanest little two-bit pissant hog thief from back in the Texas timbers can come out here and be an important sonofabitch. Where else could he throw down a peon woman in the brush and have greasers bowing and tipping their hats and saying

'*Si, señor!*' every time he ordered his horse fed or some wood chopped? Man, you watch this country grow! It will build and grow from here to the Chisos Hills when all the crud in Texas assembles out here—Now I got other people to see—"

"Doc—what's the posse doing next? Have they ridden out yet?"

"Never mind. You're through with that. You're out of action from here on. Till I say different."

"I feel all right."

"Near concussion. A serious thing. We had an expert talk on it at Fort Worth, last medical meeting I went to back east. Good thing I learned a little about concussion and skull fracture. This is a country that has them in epidemics."

"Such as Taggert? He must have died before you went to the medical meeting."

"Uh-huh. When I get all this country I can stand, I take out, maybe once a year. Long ways back to civilization and not many ever get to make it. But I go to Fort Worth now and then and everybody has to postpone their ailments till I get back." He padded to the street with Kelly's glance thoughtfully following him.

Alice Mendoza came out of the gloom of the hallway, carrying a broom. "I've been straightening the rent rooms. Saul, how do you feel?"

Before he could speak, light footsteps crossed the walk, and Connie Wendel came in. By contrast to Alice, he saw that Connie was clean as a peach, curls just so, dress starched, lips lightly painted. She came to him and touched his arm. "Saul—are you all right now?"

Nita showed in the hallway, behind Alice, and now Jimmie came in at the front. He said, "Doc says to keep you in bed. And it's time for the green pill."

The room was too crowded. Three women—two of them Mexican—and the pen boy, and out of sight and needing some thinking about, a man named Taggert who talked on his way to dying. Kelly reached across the counter and opened the drawer. He palmed the deputy's badge with

121

four sets of eyes fastened on him. He nodded to Alice, eased past Connie, made it to the door. "Doc said I needed a dose of Ren Blankenship's medicine, Jimmie. In place of the green pill."

On the sidewalk he gulped the rancid greasewood breeze and felt steadiness return to his legs. As he walked, he pinned on Uncle John's deputy star. When he reached the Texas Bar the loiterers in front stopped their talk and curiously eyed him, then straggled in after him. The bar held a dozen or more customers. Now the sidewalk loafers joined these, and arranged themselves along the counter.

By the time he had adjusted his vision to the dimness, Kelly understood the attraction. Here was the Kelly man standing alone at the front curve of the bar, and yonder at a back table sat Shep McQuail. Both men showing matching scars and bruises from last night. Ren Blankenship moved to the counter across from Kelly. He squinted one eye and jerked his chin, a worried signal.

"I see him, Ren. Set me out a bottle."

The first uneasy silence broke along the bar lineup, as men made a show of resuming their talk and drinks, but in subdued tones and movements. Kelly turned, seeing the only vacant tables were toward the rear, where Shep McQuail drank alone. He chose the table nearest the entrance, where Jeb Mott sat. Mott's frown deepened as Kelly approached. Kelly carried the bottle and the glass, and fished back a chair with his boot.

"You mind?"

Mott looked uncomfortable and cut his glance to the back table. Kelly sat. He poured the glass to the brim and examined its amber beads for a moment, then took a tentative sampling.

"You stock good whisky, Mott."

Jeb again cast an uneasy glance the length of the gloom toward Shep at the back table.

In that moment, Shep called in a loud voice: "Ren—goddamit get over here and wipe the slop off this table! Place is a stinkin' pigpen—"

122

Kelly raised an eyebrow. "Your customer back there must have been hitting the bottle for quite a while."

Mott murmured uneasily, "Yeah, he has."

"You don't look very comfortable, Mott. Had you rather I sat somewhere else?"

Mott looked away. From the corner of his mouth he said painfully, "I'd just as soon you didn't act so damned chummy. With Shep back there."

"I thought we might talk about the Hinga property."

"Not right now. Not here. But I'll say this. I looked it over and it's not much. You be figuring your rock-bottom price."

Mott nervously inched his chair away.

"You're a little fidgety, Mott."

"I'll talk to you later. Why don't you just quietly leave, now—"

Kelly felt the hush drop over the bar lineup. He glanced to the back. Shep McQuail was unsteadily working to his feet. Shep stiffly raised his arm and downed a glass of whisky. He wiped his mouth. Swaying, he craned at the front table. "Mott! Jeb Mott! You goddam greaser-lover! Come back here where the white customers are!"

Jeb's cigar drooped and his face went red.

Kelly murmured, "I think the drunk back there is calling you."

Mott started a slow walk toward the rear with silent attention hammering rivets into every step.

"What you want, Shep?"

Shep downed another whisky. He tossed the glass to the floor. "Hi-ya, Big Boy!" he said loudly, with exaggerated friendliness. "How you feelin' after sidin' with all those greaser-lovers last night? Big show you-all put on down at the wagonyard—"

"I wasn't in that!" Mott retorted.

"Well, your daddy-in-law was!"

"Wasn't any of my doing, Shep. I wasn't even around—"

"All the town against us!" Shep made a wild sweeping

123

motion to encircle Grande Flat. "Those town bastards! Pulled guns on us. Listen to me, Mott—"

"Now, Shep, you just sit and take it easy." Mott struggled for good nature in his tone. "I wasn't with that bunch."

"Then where the hell were you?" Shep shouted. "Pouring your sister-in-law's ears full of poison about *me?*"

Mott visibly jerked. "Godamighty, Shep, I didn't have anything to do with that!"

Ren had come to stand over Kelly. He whispered in agitation, "Shep's fightin' drunk, lost his head. Why don't you just ease out of here?"

But to Kelly's alerted attention, the scene hinted at an unsuspected sore about to be uncovered. "Not yet, Ren. The curtain just now went up."

A middle-aged range man got up from a table and walked over to touch Shep's arm. "Now let's calm down, Shep," he said steadily. "Let's just take a bottle and go down to the wagonyard—"

Shep got a cross-eyed focus on the man. "Aw right, Berry." He allowed Berry to guide him a few steps away from Mott. Then he stopped, twisted back, and loosened his bruises with a leering grin. "Mott, why ain't you content with sleepin' with just *one* of the Wendel girls?"

The room froze to a man, then stayed locked from delayed shock. Kelly felt his own blood pound. The words stayed printed in the tobacco smoke, rank enough to smell like an invitation to gun powder.

Then Shep allowed his friend to guide him in a weaving course the length of the bar. He yawed and slowed a dozen paces from where Kelly sat alone. Kelly held an empty glass in his left fingers, slowly twirling it. His right hand rested palm down on his thigh. Shep worked his mouth, nothing came out, and he angrily tore his arm out of Berry's light grasp. Flinging himself ahead, he staggered for the swinging doors, struck them open with a drive of his fist and Berry followed him to the street.

At the back table, Mott shakily picked up the bottle and lifted it for a gulp that wet the front of his shirt. Holding

124

the bottle by its neck, he trudged into the rear hallway with every eye on him and vanished into the office behind a slam of the door.

Ren Blankenship mopped at his sweat, and asked Kelly, "You aiming to keep wearing that deputy badge?"

Kelly poured a drink. "Why don't you sit down, Ren? Shep's gone now. You and I really haven't had a visit."

Ren reluctantly lowered himself to a chair.

"Just curious, Ren—what was Shep's meaning to Mott, about confining himself to just one of the Wendel girls?"

Ren removed his dead cigar, looked at the soggy end, and fixed it back in his mouth. "I dunno. Something to do with Connie. She and Shep had a bustup. Just drunk talk."

"Now come on, old friend. Isn't it more than that?"

Ren squirmed uncomfortably. "Well, nothing out loud." He changed the subject. "Saul, why don't you make a quick sale to Mott and get out of town?"

"May do it—Just a small item of curiosity, Ren—who was a man named Taggert? Died after a fall off a windmill?"

Ren thought back. "He was a range hand. Worked different places."

"Did he make a trail drive to Kansas with the McQuails?"

"Yeah, recollect that he did. The drive two years ago."

"That happen before Doc Rice went back east to a doctors' convention?"

Ren thought and counted fingers. "I reckon so. Doc made his trip couple of months ago."

"What was Taggert's first name? What did they call him? Did it happen to be 'Shawnee'?"

"Joe. They just called him Joe, or Tag. What difference does it make?"

"It's nothing—which way did the posse ride this morning?"

Reluctantly, Ren said, "West, I think."

Kelly stiffened. "To the Mendozas'?"

"Listen, Kelly—why don't you leave that alone? Why you stick your badge on, that you got no right to wear, and push

125

your nose in things? This place is already on a powder keg."

Kelly thoughtfully poured from the bottle. When he did not reply, Ren glanced cautiously over one shoulder, then leaned forward. "Kelly, you haven't seen old Clabe Peabody around, have you? Since what happened to Blackie?"

Kelly shook his head, reading the deep agitation in Ren. "You think Peabody might have found out something?"

"I dunno. It's had me worried. I got to go to Blackie's funeral this afternoon. Won't hardly be anybody there. I wish you would come. I just don't like to be out and around, with maybe old Peabody on the loose, half crazy, no telling what he's heard, where he might show up."

Kelly thought of Alice Mendoza, and said, "Guess I won't make it to Blackie's funeral. I had my quota of funerals yesterday—What did Bert and his crew plan to do at the Mendoza place?"

Ren hesitated. "Talk I heard in here, they plan to burn something. The barn or a Mex shack. Just a demonstration to get even for Blackie, warn the greasers. Maybe scare some of that bunch out of the country."

It was more than a Mendoza barn they planned to burn, and the man who just then hurried through the batwings was pleased to be the first to make the announcement. He braced at the bar, motioned for whisky, and loudly addressed the crowd: "The posse burnt Mendoza's house. They pulled Miz Mendoza outside fightin' 'em like a wildcat and then carried Mendoza out on his cot, broke leg and all, and plunked him down in the yard, then poured the coal oil and set the house afire. I guess we've seen the last of *that* bunch of *tamales*."

It had taken Kelly half an hour to return to the station pen, get his horse saddled, and ride to Coyote Creek crossing. When he pulled up there, listening, he heard a band of horsemen approaching from out of sight in the upgrade mesquites. The posse was returning to town. He spurred his horse into the downstream creekbed and rode beyond the first bend. He stayed in concealment until he heard the

126

riders cross the shallow. When distance absorbed sound of them, he rode west again, threading through the trees off the road.

Suddenly, his horse flattened its ears and pumped its neck in a seizure of nervousness. Kelly caught the first whiff of the fire smell, a crawly thing creeping out of the brush. A moment later he saw the snake of dirty smoke invading the bland skyline.

After half a mile, he broke out of the brush near the east edge of the Mendoza clearing where the silent scene stopped him abruptly, his stomach turning hollow. The only movement was made by the rising smoke from the fallen-in house in the background and by the flames still nibbling within the jumble of blackened debris. The heat-tilted adobe walls formed a jagged, charred skeleton with burnt-out eyes that had been windows, and encased the still burning jumble that had been roof and furnishings. The tree leaves had fried brittle and the limbs were charred on the row of chinaberries that had shaded the porch.

A distance back in the open, Ferd Mendoza lay under a quilt on an iron cot that stood in a patch of broomweeds and trampled bluebonnets. Beside the cot, Maria Mendoza sat in a wooden straight chair, as motionless as Mendoza, her back to the mesquites, her head facing the house. Her hands were folded in the lap of her full dark skirt. Her black hair played in breeze-caught strands from the loosened knot at the back of her neck. The only movement by either of them that Kelly saw was when she bent forward once and fanned at the gnats above Mendoza's head.

At the workers' shacks in the distance, he saw a few immobile figures standing in the shadows, watching. Back on the main road to the south, he saw a few lingering spectators, curiously taking it in from the fringes of the mesquite thicket.

He dismounted and walked to Señora Mendoza. She glanced up dully. He stood beside her chair and she suddenly stood, and drew him close with an emotion-flooded embrace, planting her head on his chest. Her shoulders shook, then she released him and wiped at her eyes.

A rider dismounted on the road and walked forward from the distant scattering of the curious spectators. He aimlessly moved about in the yard, looking over the ruins. His jerky stalking brought him nearer, for a hard look at Ferd on the cot and at Maria and Kelly. He was a rough-garbed, stocky man, wearing old-fashioned knee-high boots and a flat-top hat as stained and weathered as his gray-stubbled jaws. The squint he locked on Kelly was a range man's crabbed ice-blue scrutiny.

"You figurin' to move 'em out of the weather?"

Kelly nodded, wondering if he was supposed to know this tough chunk of old cactus. "Yeah. I figured to."

Ferd Mendoza raised to his elbow. He motioned toward the workers' quarters. "I'll not burden the houses of my people. They don't want us down there. They're afraid."

Cactus-face nodded his understanding of that. He planted calloused thick hands in each hip pocket and stared at the smoking ruins.

"Had a house burnt on me once," he said gruffly. "Comanches did it. They killed my wife first, then burnt my cabin."

The man's expression had gone far away. Kelly said quietly, "If you would help me get a wagon hitched, mister—"

Without replying, the man ambled toward the pen. He yelled in grating Spanish for some of the workers to bring a team for the wagon.

Kelly heard a new arrival riding out of sight on the road, the horse sending ahead the thuds of galloping hoofs. He scanned the road in heightened anxiety.

When she came into view among the mesquites, she made a slight figure in the saddle, with her skirts bunched above her bare knees. She stopped when she first saw the ruins, and her parents in the clearing. She left the horse and advanced in controlled steps to stand beside Maria's chair. Maria reached and found her hand. Alice spoke to the stoic man on the cot. "Are you all right, *padre?*"

Ferd made a taut smile. "Been a little warm, for May."

128

She moved a small brown hand absently to smooth her hair into place. Included with the movement was a quick rub across her eyes, and only the long lashes showed moisture shining in the sunlight.

Maria stared at the ruins and spoke softly, "It was our home."

Alice shaded her eyes, as if seeking to identify the twisted blackened remains of things remembered. "Yes, that was all, *madre*. It was just our home that the white men burned."

The stocky man with the stickery whiskers came back and fed a bite of tobacco into the hole of his cactus growth. An introduction seemed called for and Kelly said, "My name's Kelly. John Hinga's nephew."

The man planted his hands in his hip pockets again. "Yeah. Stayed at your place last night. Come over to see Hinga and get my horse. Found the town full of commotion. Name's Feeney. Mack Feeney. North Arroyo."

Feeney called out a few curt words of direction to the Mexican who had driven up the wagon. The Mexican made adjustments to the harness and started back afoot to the shacks along the ravine.

"They don't want to get mixed up in it," Feeney commented bleakly.

Kelly said, "I don't expect them to. You want to take one end of the cot and help me lift it to the wagonbed?"

"Yeah. Take ahold."

They lifted Ferd into the wagon. Kelly assisted Maria to the hub and onto the high spring seat. He took the reins of the horse Alice had ridden and tied them to the tailgate. "You ride with Maria and drive the team."

Feeney had gone to bring his horse. As Kelly mounted, Feeney asked, "Where you takin' them?"

"Why, I'm taking them into Grande Flat," Kelly said. "To the stage station."

Feeney thoughtfully fingered his bristle. "Good as any. I'll ride along. Damn, ain't a house burnt an ugly thing to look at?"

Kelly reined in front of the team and led the way across

the clearing to the road. There appeared to be no spectators left in the shadows along the town road. But as Kelly searched ahead, one man took ghostly form against the brush. In the lengthening shadows of late afternoon his hair and flowing beard shone white. His old withered hands stayed busy working the bridle reins and a shotgun balanced across his saddle.

Kelly stiffened in a flood of memory and recognition. The old man pulled his horse to the center of the road, blocking the way. He worked his fingers over the tobacco-stained flow of beard. "Burnt 'em out, did they?"

"Yes, sir."

"Heard there was excitement. Word come back in the brush, so I rode in to see what was goin' on."

"Well, you're seeing, Mr. Peabody."

Peabody carefully looked him over. "I know you?"

"Saul Kelly, John Hinga was my uncle."

"Good man. Hear he went to his reward. Who's that one?"

"He's Mack Feeney, from North Arroyo."

Feeney impassively eyed the old man and spat tobacco juice and Peabody promptly matched the amber jet with a demonstration of his own. "I know. Heard Blackie Toyah stole your horse. That it?"

"This is it."

"Blackie always was a mean little cuss. Where you folks goin'?"

Kelly lifted his reins. "We're taking the Mendozas to the Hinga station for the night."

"Mexicans in the *hotel*? Godamighty, them white cow-boys will tear it apart!" He pulled his mount about. "Mind if I go along? You may need some support. Got nothing better to do. Been off trailin' a clue to the bandit that killed my brother, Pete, a long time ago. Didn't pan out and I'm needin' to rest up before I start out again."

Kelly thought of Blackie, dead, and of Ren Blankenship whose boyish terror had never quite died. He said gravely, "Be glad to have your support, Mr. Peabody."

The procession started. It wound downgrade to Coyote Creek, over the crossing, up the sandy ruts, and into the outskirts of Grande Flat. Kelly rode in the lead. Next came the wagon with Alice driving, Maria on the high seat beside her, and Ferd on the cot in the open wagonbed. Trailing the wagon, Feeney rode his recovered horse, and trailing Feeney on his swayback blue mustang was Clabe Peabody with his whiskers blowing and his shotgun across his saddle.

Kelly called, "Take the turn behind me, Alice. The main road. We're going all the way down main street to the station."

She called an urgent protest, but he ignored it. And that was the way Grande Flat saw the strange arrival in the early dusk.

First they had to pass the wagonyard. A form of cold hate took hold in him. He shifted weight to the left, bringing the sixgun butt up to graze his right fingers. One man had stopped outside the gate. Kelly recognized Shep McQuail. Shep stared with his mouth open. Then he called excitedly: "Bert! Com'ere!—Strawn!—Strawny-y!—Hey, *Strawny-y!* Come look—!"

Strawny!

Kelly's blood pounded, washing him with memory. The low, excited call in the Territory night, the exact tone, and the word. Not *Shawnee!*—as he had vaguely believed. *Strawny-y!* It had been Shep's excited call to Strawn during the ambush. His fog of memory lifted, the puzzle cleared. He knew "Shawnee" was identified at last.

The procession moved on. He glanced back as men straggled out of the wagonyard. He saw Bert, Strawn, a dozen others, staring. The saloon next emptied out its customers to the porch. The store doorways and walks sprouted craning necks. Kelly saw them as a blur while his mind kept ringing *"Strawny-y!"* He turned at the side alley to the Hinga pens.

A long high yell like a battlecry sounded south at the wagonyard, followed by a gun blast.

Kelly assisted Maria and Alice from the wagon. Feeney and Peabody hurriedly went to the tailgate and hoisted Mendoza out on the cot.

Maria's mouth was working at something between a smile and a sob. On impulse, Kelly bent and kissed her cheek. "Don't be afraid. You should feel right at home here."

Jimmie came, popeyed, to help unhitch and get the horses in the pen. When he was aside with Kelly for a moment he said in agitation, "Mexicans ain't allowed rooms in Grande Flat, Mr. Kelly."

Kelly said something noncommittal. His mind still played uneasily with the fleeting glimpse he'd had of Strawn's expression. As they had passed the wagonyard, Strawn had stared at Kelly as if seeing a ghost. Then he had tugged at Bert's arm and said something to Bert from the corner of his mouth.

The expected message came as Kelly, Feeney, and Jimmie finished feeding and watering the livestock. Two men, unknown to him, trudged down the alley and confronted Kelly as he came out the gate. One of them spoke without preliminary: "Kelly? We've brought a message from the posse. A white man was murdered and the posse burnt that house to teach the greasers a lesson. They don't aim for you to un-teach it. You've got till noon tomorrow to get those damned greasers out of here."

They turned and walked off before Kelly could form a reply.

10.

An uneasy night settled down upon the uneasy town. A scattering of late-arriving riders, tardy in getting word of a manhunt, showed up and began to slake their thirst at the saloon and to try to get the straight of what was going on. Bonfire smoke curled again at Minnow's corral. The street secured its doors and the town people disappeared.

Kelly surveyed the dark and deserted street from the front of the stage station. Then he brought in his saddle carbine and rested it against the wall at the office counter, with a box of ammunition beside it. Mack Feeney had placed his own rifle within reach at the side window. Clabe Peabody selected a chair and located his shotgun on the floor after first working a dirty bandana over it as gently as cleaning a baby.

In the back room at the Texas Bar, Jeb Mott sat dejectedly in a whisky stupor, nursing a gnawing resentment against Shep McQuail. He knew that a compulsive design for this night worked in the back of his head, but he was not going to rush it. The whisky bottle kept whispering that Connie was alone tonight, that Otto Wendel had gone to the Hunt Goodman ranch for the night, that Mrs. Wendel was due home on the stage tomorrow.

Wendel himself sat in a shallow ravine off the south

133

road, two miles from town, resting with his back against a boulder. His horse cropped grass nearby, and Wendel occasionally struck a match and looked at his watch.

In one of the small bunk rooms in Minnow's sprawling barn, Bert McQuail sat on a cot edge with a whisky bottle in his hands, facing Shep and Strawn. It had taken the past half hour to get Shep roused enough to hear serious talk.

"Pa sent word in," Bert was saying petulantly. "Jim Riker came and said Pa's on a mad high-horse. All that on top of that goddam Kelly."

Strawn asked sourly, "What's Brack's ailment?"

"He says for us to come home *pronto*, to break this up. He laid the law down."

Shep mumbled, "On a real mean streak, huh?"

"Yeah." Angrily, Bert added, "You had to go put on a big drunk. Now you got Jeb Mott down on us and that probably means Wendel, too. We're in big trouble and you ain't going to be any help." To Strawn he said hoarsely, "Now we've got to take care of this thing. If Kelly is who you say he is, we're in a right bad fix. Right bad."

Strawn's slack mouth worked. "No doubt in my mind. But no use to get spooked about it. We're not sure *he* knows."

Bert said urgently, "You *positive* it's Kelly? You recognized him?"

"Would bet a million. When he rode in tonight with them greasers—when I got a better look—hell, I *know* he's the man I saw in Abilene. I *saw* those two get the money at the bank that time. And that knife slice—by God, that settles it. It all come back to me like it was yesterday. Boys we're in boilin' water and its name is Arbuckle Canyon."

"Oh, hell," Shep moaned. "Oh, goddamit everlastin' to hell. Pa will kill us!"

Bert felt like moaning, too. He almost wished he was as drunk as Shep. He spoke painfully to Strawn: "We're all in this together. Now we ought to be able to take care of just one man."

134

Strawn carelessly flicked his thin fingers. "Well, you're the brains. You schemed it the other time. Now figure how to get Kelly set up and we'll take care of the gent."

"More than him," Shep mumbled. "What about that feller Feeney down there? And that old hermit with the shotgun?"

"Well, we got us a fair-sized force of vigilantes here," Bert said thoughtfully. "This crowd's come a long ways and they're keyed up to want some action before they go home. I think tomorrow they'll be ripe to bust in that stage station and pull those Mexicans out of there. And when we do that—we take care of Kelly."

Strawn murmured, "My pay, Bert. You been owin' me a long time. That Mendoza freighting business—when you comin' across with that, Bert?"

"Hell, ain't I workin' on it by ever' means possible? You'll get it. After today, it's just a matter of puttin' the pressure on and the Mendozas will leave the country."

Doc Rice emerged from the station hallway. "Ferd's bedded down. His leg wasn't damaged. In a day or two he can get around on crutches." He frowned. "What is this— fortin' up for a stage?"

"That will be up to the posse," Kelly replied.

"Quite a military force you've got here. I reckon you know the whole town's on edge."

"You pass the word, Doc. Any of the town men that feel moved to join us, they will be welcome."

Rice mopped his face. "Well, you paraded a challenge, way you brought 'em in here. You know this could turn into—into a civil *war?*"

Feeney said flatly, "Folks that have always been on the fence had better get ready to be shook off, one side or the other."

Doc stubbornly wagged his head. "Bunch of white Yankees tried it like this once back in East Texas, I recall. They took a nigger family to the safety of the courthouse

135

for this kind of protection. So the mob just burned the courthouse *with* the niggers and *with* the whites and shot the ones that tried to run—"

"I heard of that," Kelly remarked. "The mob had on masks and bed sheets and carried a burning cross, so that made it patriotic. Now we have the border version of the same thing, out here in the last little place on earth. Grande Flat. Just the bed sheets missing. That would scare the horses in this country. The Mendozas' house was the burning cross."

Feeney said, "The McQuails didn't need to burn the Mexican house. A house set afire does something bad to me. Blackie Toyah wasn't worth the sorriest sod shack in the country. Those McQuails have got the gall of a hyena," Feeney went on, seized with the rare talking streak of a man amidst listeners after long living alone. "I recollect seeing them once in a gambling house in Kansas. Reckon they stayed over in Abilene having a go at the cards after selling a herd. They were livin' high. I didn't know 'em except by name, but they sure hogged the spotlight for a day or two."

Kelly held veiled attention on Doc Rice and prompted, "How'd they come out, Feeney? With the gambling?"

"Big winners, the first day. You'd thought they owned Abilene. But nobody ever beat those market-town dives for long. Heard later they not only lost their winnings, but their whole roll from the cattle sale. I wondered how they would face up to old Brack with his money lost. They tell me he's a stripe that would shoot his own sons for a thing like that."

Kelly noticed Doc's hands fumbling and spilling tobacco as he tried to load his pipe.

"Doc, will you come back to the shed a minute? Would like for you to take another look at this head knot."

Sure that Doc would follow, he caught up his rifle, unbolted the door and called back, "Lock it after us, Feeney, and you and Peabody keep your eyes on things, will you?"

He walked around the side of the building and into the

136

pen. He lighted the lamp in the shed room. He saw the note on the table, the pencil-printed instruction Doc Rice had left for Jimmie: *White pill one hour, green one the next, cold water bandage and ointment in between.*

He hardly needed to make the comparison. But he pulled the anonymous note from his wallet and looked at the two side-by-side under the lamp. Doc Rice came inside and his attention at once settled to the slips of paper in Kelly's hands.

He cleared his throat. "Well, let's see that wound."

"The wound's all right, Doc. It's just a question or two that needs a scalpel." He thrust the two notes at Doc who instinctively drew back, not touching the paper slips.

Kelly thought of all his fruitless trails and travels for months past, the false leads and the dead ends. He was unable to keep bitterness out of his voice. "You're a man that fair likes to have a thing done the hard way, Doc. This business concerns men robbed, one of them murdered, a long stretch of time gone out of my life, looking, hunting, forever working on it. And here it was, Doc, right back practically on the doorstep of this goddam shed room, where I used to live, where we are right now. Right here on this cot where Taggert died. Died talking of Arbuckle Canyon." He touched his thin white scar. "You could have saved me a lot of time, Doc. The end is going to be the same, anyhow."

Doc's jaw knots churned in agitation as he forced a slitted glance up to the big man towering over him. "What end—?"

"Why, somebody's got to die, Doc. How could it be any other way? I don't see those three meekly submitting to arrest and sedately riding three hundred miles to Austin for a federal trial. Do you?"

Doc bristled up like a cornered badger. "I don't know what you're talking about! I don't know now and I never am going to know, and that's going to be my damned story till Kingdom Come!" His tone sagged, sapped of its bluster. "They got to die, you say?"

"All three. Bert and Shep and Strawn. Them or me. I asked you—you know any other way out of it?"

"No. I reckon not."

"You going to leave it like that? You're not going to tell me about it?"

Doc stared unblinking. "I told you I don't know what you're talking about."

Kelly shrugged. "Then suppose I put it together for us. The McQuail boys blew their old man's money in an Abilene gambling hall. Then they hired Strawn because they needed his kind of help and headed for the Indian Territory, pushing day and night on the trail of a pair of riders they heard were traveling to Texas with cattle money. Taggert was the fourth man in that fine quartet, and they jumped their quarry one night in Arbuckle Canyon. Dick Hubbard and Saul Kelly. So the son of the Governor of Texas died on the spot and I was just lucky to get this knife slice across my face and a bullet burn across my shoulder and fall out of sight over a cliff. Then the McQuails came home, and like dutiful sons they turned over to Brack the three thousand dollars cash payment on the herd sale. Likely they never knew who it was they murdered. Then, one day Taggert fell off a windmill and before he died he jabbered to you about Arbuckle Canyon. I guess that didn't mean anything to you, at the time. But you went east to the doctors' convention and that's where you linked it up. Fort Worth. Back there in civilization people knew Dick Hubbard had been murdered in the Arbuckle Mountains—that Dick and his friend, Saul Kelly, had been ambushed, the cattle money stolen. You heard about it, and you added things together. You came home and it got to gnawing you, because you had a damned good lead on the mystery that every federal lawman in the east was straining his guts to solve. Time came when you couldn't sleep good. You remembered the Kelly boy, the nephew of your old friend, John Hinga. You heard in Fort Worth that I was a federal marshal in Austin. So it ate you—and one day you felt compelled to do a *little* something. Not go all the way, mind

138

you, just enough to salve over your conscience. Nothing big and bold and forthright—you would take care of it all by sending that tricky little note, and then sit back and see if the Kelly boy could work it out for himself—"

"Now goddamit, Kelly, that's enough of that!" Doc sat haggard, his hands shaking. "I'm not going to say that I did and I'm not going to say that I didn't. There's just this I'll say—" His belligerence faded. "My whole life has been spent trying to keep people from dying—not *killing* them. And there's more than that—" He stopped.

"What else?"

"Taggert wasn't the only one I've seen die, Kelly. Not by a long shot. And not the first one to talk out of his head while he was about it. A *lot* of 'em do that. Now that's where a doctor has got to draw the line and he learns this early when he begins to see 'em die on him." Rice examined his pale fingers, not looking up. "What he's got to do, Kelly— he's got to decide how much of what he hears is in confidence. No, not that, exactly—I mean, when it comes to that stage, when a mortal is half here on earth and half not, stepping across to that other world—at that express moment, son, I have come to accept it that he's talking to God. Not to me, to *God*. For all I know, he's already seeing Him." He jerked up a strained and searching gaze. "Do you understand? The doctor's got no right to go blabbing off a private conversation he accidently overheard, that somebody about two breaths from death was having with his Maker, the Man he already might be shaking hands with and getting acquainted with, for all I know, and telling Him how it was, something that happened down here. Well, what they were talking about dies with 'em, far as I'm concerned."

"And that's how it was with Taggert?"

"I'm not going to admit one cussed thing! But—well, Taggert, for instance. There was a man going out and trying to talk fast at the last minute, to explain something that bothered him. Well, maybe later on, a doctor remembering that, and then hearing something else that linked up—

Lord, it would put him in a predicament! Was he going to be a mouthpiece for a dying Taggert, or was he just going to do the least possible, a gesture at another kind of duty—and nothing more?"

"Maybe I follow you, Doc. A little way. I suppose it was your decision, if you wanted to call it a deathbed confession—"

"Now I'm not settin' myself up to be a priest, Kelly! Nobody was confessing to *me!* What I heard, like I told you, I was just somebody that happened to overhear a conversation between—between the party of the first part and—" he jerked a thumb toward the ceiling—"and the Party up there."

Kelly said, "Dick Hubbard died, too. Remember that."

Rice laced his fingers and stared at the floor again. "Kelly, there's another thing. In my work I'll look inside a man's belly and down his gullet and up his ass, but be damned if I pry into his soul. Every man's entitled to at least one private, personal secret in his life. Good or bad, it's his alone. To mess around in it, without his leave, that's unholy *intrusion.* Even Taggert." He swept his arm. "Even the people in this putrefied-scab corner of Texas, or anywhere."

Rice got up and fixed a grim stare on Kelly, then his harsh expression softened. "There's another secret, but a horse of a different color. You can be bracing yourself for it. When it comes, you might remember what I've just said."

"Well, name it, Doc."

"John Hinga's will is in my office safe. I witnessed his making it a long time ago. It's not five lines long but it says all he wanted to say. Soon as we can get at it, I'd better pull it out and read it before the people concerned."

Kelly felt only indifference to Uncle John's will. Nothing existed but the cold hard lump in his stomach of knowing the old mystery of Arbuckle Canyon had been cleared. That —and Bert and Shep and Strawn and trail's end here in Grande Flat. His mind raced ahead to the final task, the odds against him, the uncertainty as to what help he could expect in this uneasy village.

140

Rice worriedly asked, "What's next with you, Kelly? How do you go about it?"

Kelly rolled the pencil notes together and inserted them in his wallet. "Like I said, I don't figure those three would respond to an engraved invitation to come to the Austin jail. My job is simply to arrest the two McQuails and Strawn on a federal charge of murder in the Oklahoma Territory. Since I don't expect they'll arrest easy, the next step—well, it has to be whatever way they force it to be done."

Nita served a delayed supper, and afterward Kelly was in a back room cleaning his six-gun when Alice quietly entered. He had removed the rounds and was wiping each load before replacing them in the cylinder. Alice halted at sight of what he was doing.

"Saul?"

He placed the gun on the dresser. "Come on in."

She cautiously advanced. He thought, *Here's one who's had her share and more of a bad time she never invited.* Gently he caught her shoulders and kissed the lips of her upturned face. She yielded and clung to him for a moment. Then, belatedly startled, she drew back and stared up to him with her dark eyes wide and shining.

"Why you do that?"

"Why *did* you do that—quit dropping words when you're shocked. Why, it just came to me that I've been intending to. For six years or more."

"Oh! The shy boy has gotten bold in his old age!"

"I dunno. Had a bold spell once in my youth, as I remember."

She blushed. "This is no night for jokes to be made! I want to know—what is going to happen, Saul? We are not —none of us are comfortable to be here. We do not wish to be cause of more trouble for you."

"Would Ferd and Maria have been more comfortable through a night in the brush? These are public lodgings."

"My father has decided. He says this is no country for us.

141

He wishes to send word to Bert McQuail that he will sell the business. Then we will move back across the border."

"Not yet, Alice. Not for a while."

Her lips tightened. "There is something else. Our little plan has not worked out so well, Saul. Connie Wendel *knows!* When she came back this afternoon she as much as told me. What she saw that night, and the dress from Nita, and the cloth she smelled burned in the kitchen—"

He had been afraid of that. But wanting to reassure Alice, he said, "I think I can take care of Connie—"

"Yes, I just expect you can, Saul Kelly!"

He looked at her oddly; her small body appeared to bristle. "Well, what does she intend to do about it?"

"She wishes to talk with you. You are to go to her house tonight. She is alone there. She made a point of that!" Her eyes flashed. "I would guess she will want to bargain—that she would like for you to take her away from Grande Flat. But perhaps you will be pleased to make a trade like that, no?"

He gave that some thought as he turned and completed the reloading of the heavy Colt. Alice watched in silence as he methodically tied down his holster to his thigh with a rawhide strip and tried the feel and position of the gun butt.

He straightened and smiled down at the pinched and anxious features. She whispered fiercely: "I should not say this—but I will hate every *step* that you take when you go to see her—"

" 'A man must accept his fate.' "

"Ah! Seneca said that!"

"Yeah." He grinned. "He was a greaser. He couldn't have gotten a room in this town nor have bought a meal at Curley's."

Her eyes shone, reaching across to Kelly like a caress. "Yes, a Spanish school teacher turned Roman. Your books, Saul. Mr. Hinga let me take them home after you left. I read them all, many times. I wanted to know what *you* had known—" Her voice trailed off. She whispered miserably,

"The books burned. They were in the fire with everything else."

Mack Feeney tapped cautiously, then pushed the door open and stalked in. He squinted in curiosity from Kelly to Alice, and back. "Things seem a little too quiet out in town Kelly. Makes me jittery. I always liked to make a little scoutin' around before beddin' down in Indian country."

"I'm going out now to do that very thing, Feeney. Will you and Peabody keep a watch on things here?"

Feeney nodded. He ran an impassive glance over Alice. "That time the Comanches burnt my cabin, they killed my wife. She was a Mexican woman." He turned and slouched out on his run-over boots.

From the darkened kitchen Kelly slipped into the night and heard Feeney bolt the door behind him. He made his way through the darkness of the alley alongside the horse pens. He followed a back path until he reached the brush-covered vacant block that afforded a partial view of main street as well as the wagonyard gate to the south. He settled in cover, blotting himself out in the scrub cedars. The night hung still and black, with just a few stars out, and small undefinable sounds floating in from toward the street. This was more comfortable and familiar to his feel, alone and on watch in the open instead of within the confines of a house. Over the years he had learned that a patient man concealed in the night could begin to see the invisible and read his bearings from silence and shadows in a way impossible behind a wall.

The night dragged along on its slow and troubled appointment with tomorrow. The fire glow dulled behind Minnow's row of stables. The windowpanes went dark in the Texas Bar, a final pronouncement to the official close of Grande Flat's day. Kelly silently changed positions to ease his stiffness, grateful for the signs of surface peacefulness. Evidently the McQuail force intended no violent move against the stage station this night. In that moment he caught sight of a moving shadow, scarcely more than a

143

fragment of the night. It materialized at the rear of the saloon building and floated south in the alley.

Kelly silently worked his way through the growth until he neared the back alley. Listening intently, he located the direction of the footsteps. He followed the sounds, keeping within the fringe of the trees. A block beyond, the shadow moved out of the alley and floated on toward the dark street. Kelly followed, near enough to keep the shadow in sight. The unknown one began a long diagonal course and a minute later Kelly could see that it aimed for the distant Wendel house where lamplight showed behind the front curtains. Kelly crossed in a crouching jog and came to the trees outside the low fence of the Wendel side yard.

The man stood on the porch, glancing both ways up and down the dark street. The rapping of his hand at the door was audible. The door opened and the light from within momentarily exposed his features.

Jeb Mott.

At almost the same instant, Kelly made out the dark blur of a man crouched against the side of the house beneath a window. He held his breath and froze his movements; he had almost blundered into the second man. His blood thundered through his brain, pumping the realization that the night had not been so innocent as it appeared. What manner of trap had Connie Wendel set for him?

At the knock on the door, Connie arose from the parlor sofa, quickly looked at herself in the wall mirror, fluffed her hair, and walked to the door with a small smile set on her lips. Expectantly, she opened the door and prepared to form the words, "Come in, Saul." She drew back with a gasp of surprise.

"Oh! It's you, Jeb! What is it?"

Mott pushed inside. The whisky smell was powerful. It flashed through Connie's mind that the hour was late, that Jeb had been drinking all afternoon, that she was alone in the house and Jeb knew it.

144

He gave her a clumsy pat on the shoulder and walked ahead to the parlor. She followed from the entrance hall and sat stiffly on the edge of a chair. Jeb mumbled, "Too many lights" and proceeded to blow out the one on the wall table. He sank to the sofa.

"Sit over here, Connie. I don't want to have to talk clear across the room."

She hesitated, then moved to sit on the opposite end of the sofa. He edged his weight toward her, closing the distance. He reached and covered the hands in her lap.

"You had a bustup with Shep today."

"That's true, Jeb. But I'm going to survive it."

"Had a little trouble with Shep, myself. Been a bad day. If I'm going to be accused of something, I might as well make it a fact."

"You'd better go home, Jeb. Clarice may be worried."

"Like what's here better," he said, thick-tongued. His fingers tightened on her hands. "Poor li'l Connie."

"Please don't start that again, Jeb."

"Just you and me here, Connie."

"Papa will be coming in any minute."

"Unk-uh." He wagged his head triumphantly. "He's spending the night at Hunt Goodman's ranch. Just you and me here, Connie. The last night before your ma comes home. Be sweet to me, honey."

He sensed her angry refusal forming. The whisky drugged him. He wished that his mind was clearer. There was a hold over her, if he could think how to use it.

"You love your mama and papa, Connie? You love Clarice?"

She studied him, recalling that he had begun something like this before.

"What are you driving at?"

"There's something—"

The procedure he should take now almost eluded his brain. He knew that this was not the way, yet the secret was a great power and forced him to keep on. "A bad

145

thing. 'Way back. I know about it. Not saying. Not if you're sweet to me. I mean tonight—now."

"What are you talking about?"

"There's something—would disgrace us all. Everybody named Wendel. We got to be one big lovin' family."

He worked a heavy arm over the sofa back and closed his hand on her breast. She steeled herself to stay unmoving. An old intuition came alive, its roots reaching far back into her girlhood, a wonder never quite formed, a mystery never answered.

Through set teeth, she said, "Jeb, you have some kind of power over Papa, don't you? What is it?"

"You wouldn't want to know, honey. You got the chance to save them. Let's just be on their side. *Our* side. Whole family. Got to be lovin' to one another."

She controlled a panic to spring erect. "It's something bad, isn't it? It must be, for you to take this chance. What if I told Clarice?"

"You won't tell anybody. You know better."

"Jeb, you're a fool—!"

"Not a fool to want you. Been hungry for you a long time. By God, I'm one that gets what he wants."

She could end it at any moment, she thought. Curiosity swelled strong, even stronger than the dread of knowing. She stayed rigid as his hand worked, and whispered, "What is the trouble you speak of?"

"Connie," he mumbled in her ear, "c'mon upstairs."

"No. No!"

She smelled the whisky, and his odor of hunger, and felt his hot breath burning an inch from her face. "Jeb—is it something about Mama?"

"Something you wouldn't want to know."

"I think you are right. I don't want to know. I just want you to leave." She knew she was afraid now, and tried not to show it.

"Not before we go upstairs."

"I know this, Jeb—you don't have the slightest idea of how to—to make romance, how to get what you want—"

146

Angrily, he went for her then in crazed compulsion, both hands entrapping her, his strength smothering her slight body. She fought at his whisky-powered strength, ashamed that she had begun to cry, and for what his hands were doing. He kept mumbling, "Like all one family—"

She felt sickness for her helplessness, for the predicament that trapped her because she could never let Clarice know, nor Otto, nor anyone.

"Upstairs, Connie—"

Desperately, she thought that she might pull free and run for the front door. She said, "All right," and waited for him to free her.

They both heard with startling suddenness the heavy footsteps on the porch planking. The screen squeaked and a key turned. Dazed, Jeb sat paralyzed with his arms still locked about her. He had just begun to untangle when Otto Wendel emerged from the hall and stopped, peering at them from the parlor door. It was too late for the scene to right itself, or take disguise for anything but what it was. Mott tried to slide farther back from Connie, who was straightening her dress and dabbing at her tear-streaked cheeks. Otto Wendel saw it all, the confused movements, Connie's tears, Jeb's open-mouthed surprise. A shudder went over Wendel's gaunt frame before he stiffly turned and methodically hung his hat on a deer-antler rack.

His dead voice broke the silence. "You get out, Jeb."

Jeb snarled, "You goddam *spy!* You never went to Goodman's. You wanted to trap me—"

"Get out!"

Clumsily, Mott located his feet, weaving when he found the floor tilting and the walls whirling. Tongue-tied, he struck an unsteady course toward the entrance, circling wide around Wendel, and into the dark hallway. He thought, *What if I did get caught—that old sonofabitch can't do a damn thing!*

Wendel tiredly sat on a chair across from Connie. He stared at the rug. "You don't have to tell me. I've learned to read Jeb's mind, what there is of it. I saw from the bottom of the window yonder. He was forcing—making a threat. Tonight I trapped him. I gave him rope, and by God he's hung himself."

Two full minutes of silence erected a wall between them. She did not know how to ask, or even *what* to ask. Timidly she finally said, "Papa, what is it about us that Jeb knows?"

Like a man hurting from crushed ribs, Otto squeezed out words nearly inaudible. "We've got a bad, vicious thing on our hands. An animal. We've got to get rid of it."

"He can hurt you, Papa? Or is it Mama? What is it?"

Wendel only muttered, "We would kill a coyote if one came—"

"But not a human life!"

"Don't grant that this is human. A coyote. A mad dog, more like."

She heard trouble shaking his soul and her tears came in anguish for him. She shared his hurt in a flood of compassion. "Then I would kill the mad dog, Papa."

"And if the killing turned trouble loose, made it all public?"

"Whatever it is, Papa, we could be strong enough."

His ashen lips worked with difficulty. "I believe we could. I just believe we could."

"Would you tell me?"

"All you need to know is that we can be hurt, if he is not bluffing. We might have to move, start fresh somewhere. Clarice would be all torn up."

"I am for whatever you wish to do, Papa."

Wendel woodenly stood. "You're the strong one among us. I always said so. If a bridge is burnt, child, and we can't turn back—just remember anybody that God ever made could have done a mistake back in their life." He walked over and took his hat. "Nobody's seen me. The town's on edge and it's the best time. Just remember, I spent the night at Hunt Goodman's. I can depend on Hunt." He carefully fitted his hat to his head. She noticed the weighty bulge inside his coat pocket. She uncertainly moved to-

148

ward him, half reaching. He looked at her from lidded depths and shook his head. He muttered vaguely, turned and walked to the entrance, increasing his gait as he approached the door.

11.

Mack Feeney had stood the dawn watch.
He called, "Kelly!" and Kelly roused from
his blankets in the station's front room.
Across the gloom he could see the shape of Clabe Peabody,
similarly bedded, and Feeney standing at a window.

Feeney called again and Kelly replied, "I heard it," and
pulled his Colt.

Somewhere in the distant dawn the muted urgency of
voices crackled. Running feet beat a plank walk, stroking
a drum-roll introduction to Grande Flat's new day.

Clabe Peabody swam up from sleep and yelled, "Are
they attackin'?" He first yanked his shotgun to his arms,
then put it down to fuzzily grope for his boots.

"No attack," Feeney said. "Something else."

Kelly strapped his gunbelt and crossed to the door, thinking that by rights the messenger should be Lefty Duncan
who had established a kind of priority for the role.

The jogging boots crossed the gallery. A fist hammered
the door and Kelly swung it open. The panting man was unknown to him and Kelly thought *You weren't on the job,
Lefty*.

"You Kelly? The new deputy?"

"That's right. What's the trouble?"

"Man's been murdered! Jeb Mott!"

Back of Kelly, Feeney grunted, "Well I be damn!"

"Yep. A feller found him in the brush behind the saloon alley. Shot twice."

Kelly showed surprise, and asked, "Any idea who did it?"

"There's talk that Mott had a row in the saloon yesterday with Shep McQuail. *Woman* trouble. The worst kind there is."

Kelly nodded. "That's a fact. I was there, myself. Must have been twenty witnesses. Where is Shep?"

"He's with those hardcases campin' at the wagonyard."

"Has anyone gone to break the news to Mott's wife and Mr. Wendel?"

"Yeah. Poor girl will be tore to pieces. Somebody's riding to get Wendel. He's out at Hunt Goodman's place." The man asked cautiously: "You aiming to arrest Shep for murder?"

Kelly put on a thoughtful look. "If he has an alibi for last night, he may want to come see me and clear himself. You can pass the word on that I'm willing to hear his side, if he's got any."

"Gossip's already running knee-deep. Wouldn't surprise me if it busts up that tough bunch playin' posse." The man peered past Kelly and asked, "Who're them two?"

"Deputies Feeney and Peabody."

The man looked impressed. "Pretty strong force. Hear the boys gave you till noon to get those Mexicans out of here."

"You take word to the McQuail outfit—if they feel moved to take over management of this stage station, they'll meet a right warm contest."

The man departed with almost as much news as he had brought.

Feeney was curiously eying Kelly. "I heard two shots off somewhere in the night. That was before you came back."

"I heard them," said Kelly. "I supposed it was only some drunk cowhand shooting at the moon."

Peabody called, "Good mornin', miss." Kelly turned to see Alice in the hallway. She replied, "Good morning, Mr.

Peabody," and held her attention on Kelly until he came to her. "Saul, did I hear that someone has been killed?"

"Jeb Mott. He was ambushed last night."

She pressed her fingers to her lips. He added, "There's talk that Shep McQuail is a good prospect."

"Poor Clarice!" And, in a whisper, "Poor Connie!"

"You know about the gossip."

"Saul—did you see her?"

"I didn't get around to it. I was keeping a lookout on that bunch at Minnow's." He saw her anxiety. "Don't worry any more about Connie. The shape of the bargain's changed a little since last night." He left that unexplained, noticing that Feeney and Peabody were curious listeners.

"Saul, my parents have been talking it over. All this violence! They wish to leave the country. My father will accept whatever Bert McQuail will pay. It is too much to longer fight, he says. We have no right here. Mexicans do not enter hotels as guests in this country."

He knew the truth of that. He could understand how the new troubles might have killed the last resistance in Ferd Mendoza. "Well, that's a decision for Ferd and Maria and you. But sooner or later there's going to be a change in the McQuail picture here and it might ease Ferd's situation a little."

"I'm hungry!" Clabe Peabody suddenly announced. "When's breakfast around here?"

Kelly smiled. "I think I hear Nita back in the kitchen. Alice, will you ask her to serve us all in the big dining room? Places for Deputies Feeney, Peabody, and Kelly, all the Mendozas, and Jimmie. The northbound stage runs today and we've got work to do, posse or no posse. Feeney, let's open the door and shutters. I'd like for this place to look inviting to Shep McQuail, in case he wants to come denying he waylaid Jeb Mott."

It was a slim chance, he thought. But he had decided to try the gambit for whatever advantage it might produce. If Shep felt the pressure strong enough, outraged innocence might push him to come state his alibi to the law. He could

152

only await developments as to whether Shep would rise to the bait. One McQuail in custody would be one-third of the job done.

Doc Rice entered the station, placed his bag beside his favorite chair, and trudged down the hall to the open doors of the main dining room. Seven people sat at the long table: Kelly, Feeney, and Peabody, facing the door; Jimmie, Alice, and Maria; and Ferd, who had been carried in on a straight chair. He had been located at the head of the table to give his splinted leg space, and faced Maria at the opposite end.

"Family gathering, looks like," Rice commented. He removed his hat and worked a frowning tally over them.

"What's the situation out in town?" Kelly asked.

"Consternation and befuddlement! A stampede of rumors. Grande Flat's one big case of stomach colic."

"Have you seen Clarice Mott?"

"Just came from there. Poor girl's shocked, but she's rising fast to the role of being the town's grieved widow. She'll play it to the hilt, I expect. She intends for the funeral to be the biggest success of its kind Grande Flat ever had."

"What about the posse?"

"Cooled off some, I hear. They've nearly forgot Blackie Toyah needed avenging. Some of the men have pulled out of it, on account of the Jeb Mott killing. All at once big Bert has more than a Mexican chase to worry about. Shep's denying right and left he killed Mott, but even his brother is not sure. They don't know but what Shep slipped out last night and gunned him down. I think folks are expecting that Shep will be moved to come see you, peaceably."

Mendoza spoke up: "Doc, how soon can I travel?"

"Why? You going somewhere?"

"We're moving below the border. My wife and I have decided that it will be wise for us to leave here. There is no choice, and all of you know this. We have no right to rooms in the stage station. We don't want to be the cause of more violence."

"I dunno about that," Doc retorted. He was standing and blowing on the coffee mug Nita had handed him. He placed it on the sideboard and stood back as if taking a stance on a rostrum. "You might change your mind about rights."

Kelly watched him curiously, caught by some sign of peculiar purpose in Doc, who was now pulling a long envelope from his coat.

"Little job to do." Doc cleared his throat. "Want to get it over with and now's as good a time as any." He worked a finger to break the envelope's sealed flap and extracted a folded paper. He squinted over his glasses, around the table, and back to the paper in his hands.

An expectant hush came. Jimmie, who had been absorbed in watching the way Old Man Peabody fed himself through a red hole in his flowing white beard, dragged blank-faced attention up to Doc Rice. Maria Mendoza, with her black hair immaculately combed and her dark molded features outwardly serene, absently fingered the handle of her coffee mug. Ferd, at the other end, was rolling a wheat-straw cigarette paper. Alice raised questioning brows to Kelly, who shrugged, and they faced back to Doc.

"This is John Hinga's will," Rice began. "There's no lawyer around here, so I substituted. He came to me sometime back and wrote it the exact way he was set on and I kept my mouth shut and did the witnessing. I'm going to read it just like it is and be finished with my part of the job and no comment, now or ever." He scowled a challenge over the table at large and cleared his throat. "This is what it says," and he read slowly and distinctly:

I, John Hinga, being of sound mind and so forth, and meaning this to be airtight and legal, do hereby and herewith leave everything that's mine, the entire stage station property, livestock, feed supply, cash in the bank, all possessions owned by me, to Señora Maria Mendoza. (Signed) John Hinga. Witness, Robert J. Rice.

For a tight thin wire of stretched seconds, the silence was absolute. Then, Jimmie's heavy hand inadvertently jarred the knife and fork on his plate in shocking loudness and he

154

reddened boylike at his public clumsiness. Clabe Peabody was somewhere else, stroking the tip of his beard in downward pulls to his gaping shirt middle. Mack Feeney folded his thick arms and stayed absorbed with his cleaned plate.

A far-back ringing began to sound slow comprehension forming in Kelly's ears. It emerged shadowy at first, then with impact. He forced concentrated study on his coffee mug.

The new wheat-straw cigarette had been dangling unlighted from Ferd Mendoza's whisker-stubbled mouth, and his hand was arrested with a match in his fingers. He slowly raked the match under the table and almost too methodically completed the lighting. Kelly floated a veiled glance to him. The Mexican's fingers were steady. There was no fathomable expression on his deep-lined face, unless the mouth corners had formed sardonic ridges, but this was so faint it might have been from his first draw on his cigarette. Ferd's attention held strictly to handling the match and did not for a second cross to the foot of the table.

The continued silence began to shrill. Kelly carefully lifted his coffee, and with the motion he was compelled to flash a look to Maria and found confirmation.

The impassive Mexican expression stayed engraved to her features, but slow-rising color seeped to the points of her cheek bones, blood-tinting the dark brown. In the instant that Kelly allowed himself the glance, she touched her forefinger quickly to the corner of each eye. For an elusive moment he saw in them, far back, a shining light exposed. Then it was concealed as she lowered her lashes. A very gentle and private smile touched her lips.

Quickly, he switched his glance away, feeling like an intruder. He saw Alice staring at her mother, lips parted at first, then the question faded away. A delicate color came to her cheeks, matching Maria's. Then Alice busied herself with a coffee spoon, not looking at her father, or anyone.

Kelly felt relieved when Doc Rice cleared his throat again and rustled the paper, folding it and replacing it in the envelope. "Congratulations to the new owners," he said

155

gruffly. "I've got some calls to make." He reached for his hat and retreated.

Maria Mendoza arose. She murmured in English, "Will you excuse me, please, father?" and Ferd courteously replied, "Yes, of course, mother," without their glances meeting. With dignity, she crossed to the hallway, and in a moment the door of her room softly closed.

Ferd Mendoza said in an ordinary tone, "Feeney, will you and Kelly carry me into the front office? I'd like to sit out there a while."

They carried him out on the chair. Kelly took a holstered revolver and belt from a counter drawer. "Strap this on, Ferd."

The Mexican said wryly. "The proprietor protects his property, eh?"

Braced in the doorway, watching the distant street, Kelly saw a man cutting toward the station across the vacant block south. He recognized Ren Blankenship who hurried on and mounted the steps.

"Ain't it the damnedest thing, Kelly!" Ren began in a rush of breath. "I need some advice. Don't hardly know what to do, Mott murdered and everything." He mopped his oily face. "The saloon was Mott's business. The bunch will be wantin' in, and soon as they get their fill of whisky, they're apt to want to storm this place if you don't turn those Mexicans out of here. You think I ought to keep running the saloon and open up today, or what?"

"Why don't you ask his wife what to do? Or Wendel?"

"Aw, she don't know anything about a saloon. I've been looking through the safe—Mott had a box of private papers locked up in there. What you think I ought to do with them?"

"I'd suggest you take them to Wendel. He can pass them on to Clarice if they're important."

"Just want to be sure I do the right thing." Ren mopped his face again. He lowered his voice. "I guess you know everybody's saying Shep killed him. Over Connie."

156

"What's your verdict? Did you see anything last night?"

"Nope. When we closed up, he stayed in the office. He was pretty drunk."

Ren choked on his last words and gazed past Kelly. His eyes protruded and he made a rattling moan in his chest. Kelly turned.

Clabe Peabody had emerged, a white-bearded ghost in the porch shadows, his watery eyes working, his shotgun dangling from the crook in his arm. He paused beside Kelly and shifted the gun.

"This here the man we been lookin' for?"

Kelly watched narrowly, realizing that the old man was confused by earlier talk that Shep McQuail might come. Kelly was about to correct the mixup, then he hesitated, taking in the effect. Ren jerked convulsively with his mouth sprung open, and sweat beads popped.

"This him?" Peabody croaked again, motioning with his gun barrel.

On cold impulse, or perhaps it was from a small fester of leftover malice, Kelly said blandly: "Deputy Peabody, this is Ren Blankenship. The man you were asking about."

Peabody hoisted his beaked nose and glowered at Ren. "Think I've seen you somewhere before, boy—"

He began to shift the shotgun and to Kelly it seemed plain that Peabody only intended to shake hands. But Ren jerked back in a seizure of trembling. "Me?" His voice broke. "Kelly, don't let him—!"

He took quick steps backward. Then he turned and strode off the porch, increasing speed as he vanished around the corner to the alley.

"Strange kind of feller," Peabody commented.

Alice was waiting as Kelly crossed the station yard to discuss stage day work with Jimmie in the pens. She called "Saul!" and flew toward him from the kitchen steps. In a burst of emotion, she grasped both his arms. "Saul! I don't know what to say! Such a shock!"

He extended a finger and forced her chin up. "Then don't say anything. That's the safest way."

157

"But they—my *madre*—your uncle—!"

"Never mind," he said gently. "Let's don't tromp around in what might look like a weed patch to some but could have been a flower garden once to someone else." He remembered Doc Rice's words. "Alice, all humans are entitled to at least one big private secret in their lives. To meddle with it is undignified. The world already has too many self-appointed judges."

"But had you ever thought—?"

"Let's don't strain to dredge up childish recollections at this late date."

"How do you suppose my *padre* feels?"

"Now don't get yourself tied up in tangles, speculating about one thing after another. Ferd is a wise man. More than that, he's a tactful one and a born gentleman. We have to grant older people that they had their younger days once and if you want to have any feelings about that, feel glad that they did. What would we ask for people to have—lifetimes as barren as this dried-up ugly country? Let's just face away from the past and look to what's ahead." He added grimly, "There's plenty of that."

She asked in embarrassment, "You don't feel bad, about not having the property left to you?"

"Not one bit." He grinned. "Seems to me it's more appropriate, done the way it's done. Besides, I didn't come back to stay. I have another job and it's across the world from Grande Flat."

"Saul—what do you *do?*"

He admitted to himself that it was time he explained. To Alice, her parents, and even Feeney and Peabody were entitled to know his purpose. He said, "You wait inside the station until I talk to Jimmie about the chores for stage day. I want that boy finished and away from here in case there's trouble."

Feeney stood on the porch with his rifle. Kelly asked, "No caller yet?"

"Nope. Too peaceful. Makes me uneasy. The bunch is

158

chompin' in front of the saloon. It ain't opened yet."

"Then Shep's not coming, I guess."

"He likely don't care whether folks think he killed the feller or not."

"Peabody inside?"

"Yeah. He's sulkin'."

"What about?"

Feeney's eye corners crinkled. "Because I got a deputy badge and he hasn't."

"I'll fix that. He can wear this one. Come inside a minute."

Alice stood beside Ferd's chair. Maria had come to the hall entrance. Peabody glanced up sourly at Feeney. Kelly removed the badge from his jacket and said, "This was my uncle's. You put it on, Mr. Peabody. It makes you a bonafide deputy sheriff. But I don't want you ever to cock that shotgun until I say so."

Peabody clutched the deputy badge, his eyes shining like a child's. He blew on its nickeled surface and polished it on his sleeve. His stiff fingers had trouble with the pin and Alice helped him complete the fastening.

Peabody beamed all around. "Pretty, ain't it?"

Alice said, "Yes. It looks splendid on you, Mr. Peabody."

Kelly took a silver shield from his pocket. "I might as well decorate myself," he said slowly. "I think by now you have a right to know my job and my mission here. All of you have become involved in it."

He pinned the badge on his jacket. Feeney squinted. "By damn, I know what that is!"

"What is it?" Ferd asked.

"He's a Deputy United States Marshal."

Five sets of eyes fastened on him. "Now you know," Kelly said. "I came to Grande Flat on a secret hunt for something. My purpose here is to arrest the two McQuails and Strawn for murder." He added sharply, "None of you has to stay to get further involved if you don't want to."

"Ain't I a deputy sheriff?" Feeney retorted. "That bunch got my dander up when they burnt the Mendoza house."

"I'm stayin'!" Peabody snapped. He patted the shotgun and fingered the deputy badge.

Mendoza said thoughtfully, "Deputy Marshal, eh? This gets interesting. First time the United States discovered this country was out here."

Maria murmured, "The little boy who lived in the shed!" and Kelly could see that she beamed with pride in him. But he could not make out Alice's expression. His glance rested on her, waiting. "Well?"

"The map of the world!" she whispered. Her eyes searched into him, then away. "So—I suppose when it—when the trouble is finished—that you will go back somewhere far off from here—"

"Yes. To Austin. That's my headquarters—Now I have two calls to make. Something that must be done before I take up the main business. Feeney, keep a sharp watch. I won't be far away. The rest of you just stay inside."

The hour was 11 o'clock, and he departed to keep his appointment with Otto Wendel.

When he walked around the road bend to the street, he could see the men congregated in front of the saloon. Evidently Ren had not yet opened for business. He studied the vague forms but could not tell if the McQuails and Strawn were among them.

Two blocks short of the saloon he crossed to the side of the Wendel store where the front shades were drawn, went on to the back, and rapped on the door. Otto Wendel came, peered through the glass, and turned the key. He led the way back to the partitioned office. Kelly noticed the metal lock-box opened on Wendel's desk with a stack of papers beside it.

"Ren Blankenship brought this over," Wendel said in his dead voice. "Never saw him so nervous. Pale as a ghost. These are Jeb's private papers from the saloon safe. There's one in particular I wanted, and I've found it." He tapped a folded document.

160

"Is that what he was blackmailing you with? The matter you mentioned to me last night?"

That discussion had been tense and hurried, with Mott dead at their feet.

"It is," Wendel said with grim satisfaction. "The envelope was addressed to Clarice—he meant to hurt us the dirtiest possible way, but thank God this is as far as it'll ever get. Unless you want to read it."

"No, I believe not. It's your private business. No country deputy sheriff has a right to pry into it."

"Thank you. So if there's no legal objection, I'll attend to this here and now." He walked to the cold iron stove, held a match to the folded paper until the flames caught, and dropped it into the stove.

"All right, Kelly. I feel better than I have for years. What's next? Do you want to arrest me?"

"Wendel, as I told you, I followed and took your place at Connie's window last night. I got a glimpse of what was going on just before you walked in on him. And I wasn't far behind you when you caught up with Mott in the saloon alley. Maybe if I'd hurried I could have got to you before it happened instead of after, with Mott already dead and you with a smoking gun in your hand. You told me there were two good reasons—one I'd just seen on Connie's sofa and one you've just burned. To an extent then, the law as this country knows it has been carried out, and if not the law, then at least justice. It was written on every hill and canyon out here long ago that a man had the full right to protect his home and his family in whatever way he has to take to do it."

Wendel said thoughtfully, "I don't know what it was that finally forced me. It kept eating me like a disease. This all came about from something long ago. Like I told you last night, it was something we had managed to forget and the air was clean out here until *he* came along to dirty it. Then for my wife and me it was like our souls were caught in shackles and it might have been that way forever, except

161

that Jeb had to push himself farther, try to use it on Connie. That was just more than I was able to stand."

For the second time that morning, Kelly was moved to quote Doc Rice. "I'm not asking you to explain what it was. Every man's entitled to his personal secret, Wendel, and I'm not going to dig around in yours."

"Thank you, Kelly," said Wendel huskily. "What you're doing for me is too big a favor for me ever to return. But if there is anything I can do, you name it."

That opened the way for his bargain. Kelly used it, carefully selecting the method of his approach. "It's a strange thing, Wendel, how some situations are coming to a head here in Grande Flat. There's the Wendel family—you're the leading name here, the top of the list. And right at the extreme bottom, clear across the world in a way, is another family and they've got a problem, too. It's different from yours. It's just that they happen to be Mexicans. Now there's a crisis come for them, no less than the one that came to the Wendels."

He waited, studying the gaunt face. Wendel murmured, "A good family."

"Yeah. Well, you're the leading citizen. I want your help in the way this town supports and respects the new owners of the Hinga property. My uncle bequeathed it to the Mendozas. To Señora Mendoza, to be accurate. We'll just say it was in appreciation for all those years she was his housekeeper. The town can let fly with its imagination all they want to. The point is, the Mendozas have the right to take over the stage station and the Hinga business and settle here and take their place as respected business people in Grande Flat. It's going to be an interesting process, Wendel. Right here in this middle of nothing there can be a complete new change of history and custom for the border country of Texas. Thanks to Blackie Toyah and Jeb Mott and even the McQuails—although they'll never know it—they'd all turn over in their graves if they knew they had anything to do with touching it off."

162

"What you're talking about, I've seen it had to come, someday." Wendel added cautiously: "I been noticing that badge you're wearing. This is something bigger than it looks, I take it. What is it you want me to do?"

"My trade with you is that you'll lead the way for the change, the process of getting the Mendozas accepted here, and protected if necessary, and given a chance to become a dignified part of the citizenship. Ferd has quietly accomplished something with his freighting contracts that shows what kind of a man he is, even if they had to do it back in the brush outside a town that custom didn't permit them to do business in. Only people of their race entitled to residence in Grande Flat had to live in the shacks in the Mexican settlement and do manual labor for the whites, and Ferd Mendoza just wasn't cut out to live like a scared peon. Now you and Doc Rice and the rest of the substantial citizens can throw some hard weight and make this change work. I'm laying it out cold, Wendel. The high cards happened to fall in my hands last night, and that's the trade I'm making with you."

Wendel considered, then asked glumly, "You're speaking as a federal marshal?"

"Damn it—I'm speaking to you as one man to another. Isn't that sufficient?"

"What if it comes to violence?"

"Then meet it with violence!" Kelly retorted. "The riffraff don't own all the guns in town. You've got a showcase full."

"When do you expect the trouble?"

"It could come this afternoon. There's a kind of ultimatum passed, that the Mendozas have got to get out of town by noon."

"The McQuail pride," Wendel commented. "Those two boys just got caught in it and think they have to follow through. Trouble with them, they never were as smart as they were big— All right. You don't leave me any choice, but I don't need any. It's a trade I'll keep, and glad to. After last night I feel like I got a foot off my neck that's been pushing down a long time. I'm ready to help the next man get the foot off his."

"Then I guess our business with one another is finished. How you'll get a force organized, I'll leave to you. One thing—I assume your alibi is solid, with Hunt Goodman?"

"I got out there before daylight without being seen."

"What about your wife?"

"She'll be on the stage this afternoon from Del Rio. I will meet her and take her to Clarice and we will be the grieved family. She will have heard about Jeb when the stage stops at Goodman's place. From there on, it's just a case that our son-in-law has been murdered by a party unknown. Just Connie and me will ever know. And you, of course."

Kelly nodded. "An unsolved murder— Now, I'm going to see Connie on a private matter, and after that I've got some unfinished business of my own to attend to. The time is getting short. If it breaks out like it might, something too one-sided for me to handle—then whatever you can do to get the town men to back me will be appreciated."

Wendel nodded agreement. "I pay my debts, Kelly."

Outside the back door, Kelly paused to listen to the street sounds. He dreaded the walk that would take him to a showdown with Connie. He wondered how far Wendel would go to keep the bargain, and tiredly thought *I drove the trade the best I could.*

12.

Walking behind the business structures to avoid the street, he reached the Wendel house from the rear, wondering how many curious eyes from windows observed the stranger calling on Connie Wendel. He thought, *Blackie, you're as much trouble dead as you were alive.*

Connie came to the back door in response to his knock. He saw that her eyes were red, her cheeks pale.

"Can I talk to you a minute, Connie?"

She attempted to show inviting affability as she led him to the parlor. He sat stiffly on the sofa where he had seen Jeb Mott digging his grave last night.

"What on earth is that badge you're wearing, Saul?"

He gestured the question aside. "I heard you wanted to see me, Connie." The words came out colder than he had intended. Connie stared at the man confronting her—a stern, unshaven stranger with a scar along his cheek and a tied-down gun on his leg. Her affability collapsed. Her small-girl smile became a trembling line of apprehension.

She twisted her handkerchief. "I expected you last night."

"Yes. Alice told me."

He knew no way to walk gracefully over this thorny course and had no time to try. "I was here last night. There's a crack under that window shade. I'm forced to tell you, Connie, that it happens I know what you and your father know, as to who killed Jeb Mott. I've just had a talk

165

with Mr. Wendel. We have an understanding. Now I wish to have an understanding with you."

Her expression showed fear, then resignation. She stared wordlessly. He plunged into it. "You thought you had some idea about Blackie Toyah's death. On the other hand, now, I know the truth about Mott's death. I followed Wendel last night when he followed Mott, and I witnessed it. There's other business waiting for me in town and this is something I wanted to get settled before it starts. To just lay the cards out plain—I don't intend to have any Blackie Toyah troubles popping out to hound the Mendozas in the future. God knows they've got enough without that. And you don't want any trouble for your father over Jeb Mott. So whatever it is that each of us knows, it sort of balances off, doesn't it?"

She nodded slowly. "I suppose it does, Saul."

"You're sure you understand me?"

"It's plain. Of course I will protect my father. It's a kind of double blackmail, isn't it?"

He ignored the bitterness behind the words and got to his feet. "Shall we say, then, that we have made a trade?"

She arose with him. Her cheeks had turned pink. "You've no idea how cheap a woman can feel in this circumstance. I offered—and you didn't buy. I would have gone with you, Saul. You only had to ask."

"Then I guess our business is finished."

He paused to glance down at her face with its deep hurt showing, and remembered that something behind it was more capable and calculating than the fetching little-girl shyness in front.

"I wish it could have been another way, Saul," she said miserably.

"I might have wished that once. You were someone fresh and clean and beautiful. Nothing for the pen boy to hope to ever reach. Never dreamed the day would come when we would have to face each other over a deal like this."

She murmured thinly, "I was going to get you any way I could. I didn't expect such competition."

"Competition?"

"I know where your real interest lies. Can't you see the extremes you've gone to for her protection? A woman senses it. That's the way it is and I'll just say—good luck."

His mind quickly high-stepped in cautious avoidance of what he supposed she meant. His denial might have been visible, for Connie forced a weak smile and said, "Now don't be blind, Saul."

At the kitchen door she came close to him. "Wait a minute." She tilted her face. "Let's don't part on such a harsh note. The rest of this day is going to be trial enough." He bent and kissed her. She stood back. "Seals our trade, I guess."

"It's sealed. Good luck, yourself."

He slipped through the doorway and hurried across the yard. The sun plastered the town with a brassy noon heat, but he already was sweating. He hurried, cut through a vacant block, and came out on the street. He saw a dressed-up trio of town women turning into the gate of the Mott house, laden with cloth-covered dishes. He hastily faced away from that scene and walked toward the distant station, keeping to the east side of the long street. When he neared a point across from the Texas Bar, he heard sounds of boisterous celebration inside. He saw that the doors finally had opened for business. He paused on the shaded plank walk in front of Hank Bonham's saddlery. He absently set his hat, then numbly fingered the worn edge of his gun holster. The street looked deceptively peaceful. He saw no movement at all in the heat haze north toward the stage station. Feeney, Peabody, and Mendoza were guards enough there, for the present, he decided. He settled against the shadowed plank wall and watched the saloon. Where were the McQuails and Strawn?

Brack McQuail stood spread-legged and livid with anger, a shaken giant now glaring in a kind of sick helplessness at the downcast droop of his two silent and suffering sons. Standing apart from them, Strawn stood poised like a watchful vulture, craftily taking it in, working the invisible

167

lines that held the younger McQuails in control. Bert and Shep slouched with their weight against a wall in Minnow's corral, as if its support was needed after the vicious beating of Brack's tirade.

Brack had wasted no time after surprising them by walking into Minnow's and bellowing their names. His voice had ranged from shouted commands to cold ultimatums. Now he was worn out and bewildered. His own sons had defied him. His hold over them was gone and he had only a sinister inkling as to how or why the rebellion had occurred. He sensed that they were secretly afraid of him, as they always had been, yet they were more afraid of something else.

He had used threats and pleading, but not much pleading. He had fired Strawn in the first five minutes when Strawn had dared to butt in. During the stormy scene, a long smouldering suspicion flamed anew in Brack. There was something extremely bad here. Something invisible, like the stench of a hidden, rotting carcass. It had a hold on his boys. And somehow, he believed, the slinky-eyed Strawn was back of it. Frustration at not knowing was almost greater than his rage over their stubborn refusal to obey orders.

"Well, I've said all I know." He stared through sweat at the suffering, oversized pair who could not meet the vicious thrust of their father's glare. "I've told you to break up this damn-fool Mexican chase and get for home and back to work, and you tell me some mealy-mouthed thing about you can't quit now. It don't make sense. There's something stinkin' dead rotten around, but no use going over all that again. For the last time, I'm telling you two big thick-headed galoots to get for home *now*—and goddam I mean *right now*—or don't ever come back at all!"

Miserably, Bert mumbled, "We *can't* Pa! The bunch is dependin' on us."

That was so thin that Brack snorted his derision. "Now that's the craziest damn thing you ever said. We've been over all of that. I don't care what else you do, but when my own sons defy my orders—that's the one thing I won't tolerate."

Shep squirmed in the same misery that afflicted Bert. He raised his whisky-puffed eyes to Strawn who grinned contemptuously. Bert also looked to Strawn, a mute and suffering plea. All that Bert got for his silent appeal was a shake of Strawn's head, and Brack, seeing it, knew for a certainty that his sons were afraid of Strawn.

He could not understand it. He turned and blindly stalked for the gate. The trio stayed silent until they heard his horse trot away.

Bert sleeved his moist face. He saw Strawn, with his crazy smile fixed, enjoying their shame. The whole sorry plight was plain. Two boys from a remote range land had gone to a Kansas wild town once and had been taken by smarter men. They had floundered, over their heads and out of their element. Now payoff time had come for getting out of the trap.

"Never had such a chewin' out," Bert bleakly commented. "Strawn, I think he smelled a rat."

"Could be. But that don't change anything."

"I reckon you wouldn't wait a little longer? You can see what a bind it's put us in with the old man."

"Can't wait," Strawn replied with relentless coldness. "Not with scar-face maybe on our tails. You know what we've got to do. The Mexican business gives us the best excuse we'll ever have."

Bert thought that Strawn always had been a little insane and he did not know how to cope with him now. Numbly, he had to face it—he and Shep were prisoners of a Kansas outlaw, a killer, and there was no way out.

"Besides that," Strawn went on, "I'm damned sick of waitin' for my pay. I helped you do the dirty work and you handed all the money over to Brack to keep your own noses clean. You promised me the Mendoza freight business, to settle. It's been a long time comin' and I'm fed up workin' like an ordinary cowhand. I'm due a settlement *pronto* on Arbuckle Canyon."

169

They had no choice. Bert and Shep had admitted that between themselves. Because Strawn was the greater threat, they'd had to defy Brack. Since childhood they had feared their own father more than any other man, but the old debt must be paid to Strawn for murder in the Territory.

"I guess Pa's gone home," Shep muttered dismally. "We might as well get at it."

Bert pulled himself out of his dejected slump and set his gun holster. "All right. Let's go to the saloon and see if the boys are fired up enough to go after them Mexicans."

Strawn had a final warning. "Just remember you can't go home, you can't go anywhere till Kelly is disposed of and you pay me what you owe me. No better setup than today. What we got to do will stand up as an honest posse's honest efforts to run down a Mexican for murder of a white man. If Kelly gets a bullet for buckin' a thing like that it's just his hard luck."

A man rushed out of the saloon, hurried across the street, and called, "Hey, just a minute!" Kelly waited, recognizing the barkeep and asked, "What's the trouble?"

"Ren's took out!" Joe said morosely. "The lynch crowd has took over in there. I'm not goin' to stay around and try to deal with that crazy bunch. It ain't *my* saloon. They're gonna go after them Mex and you better be movin' 'em out."

"Ren's left, you say?"

"Yeah. Them bastards finally broke in the doors and swarmed in. Just me there. Ren pulled stakes and vamoosed. Reason the doors was locked so long—he had me helpin' bundle his stuff and loadin' a pack horse out back. Never saw a man so scared out of his wits."

"Over what?" Kelly asked; but he knew.

"I dunno. Something happened to make him near crazy. He said he was through with this town for good, was headin' for El Paso. He was shakin' so he couldn't tie a rope. You name any scared fit you ever saw—Ren Blankenship had it!"

It's name was Clabe Peabody. Kelly's mouth formed into a grin of irony. Blackie dead, Ren scared out of the country. He guessed old man Peabody's long, obsessed quest was ended, although Peabody might never know it and would keep looking until he went to compare celestial notes with Pete. The barkeep had glanced beyond Kelly, and now moved nervously. "Yonder come the McQuails. I'm gettin' away from here." He hurried down the plank walk.

Kelly saw three men coming from the wagonyard gate. For a moment he pressed flat against the shadowed wall. He was conscious of how the street was so deserted, how quiet the town had become, and the only sounds the rumble of talk inside the Texas Bar. And yonder came the three together—the unholy trio from that black nightmare in Arbuckle Canyon. His mouth went dry. Numbly, he wondered, *did they know?* Had he observed some exposure of recognition yesterday in Strawn?

A movement jerked his attention toward the station. He saw Feeney striding into the road, and he walked off the planks to meet him. Feeney came on with importance in his bearing, as if conscious of the deputy badge on his vest that reflected the sun streaks and a man's responsibilities.

As they came up to each other, Kelly said, "That's the McQuails and Strawn at the far end of the street. Their bunch has taken over the saloon. Every man his own barkeep. I guess Shep never came calling on me, did he?"

"Shep didn't but somebody else did!" Feeney puffed out his news: "Fellow rode up from the back way and walked right in without a howdydo. Their pa. Brack McQuail. He's been to see his boys down at the wagonyard and now he's in the station, waitin' for you."

"What does he want?"

"He don't say. He's in the front room, with old man Peabody sittin' in one corner and Mendoza in another and nobody speakin' to nobody else. Brack's mad and sick both, if I know the signs."

"I could have done without him," Kelly murmured. They walked toward the station. He glanced back to see Bert,

171

Shep, and Strawn filing into the saloon. "Feeney, stay outside and watch the street. I'll send Peabody and you post him to watch the back."

"All right. You be careful with old Brack. Your badge won't mean a damn thing to him."

Brack McQuail faced the entrance with his left elbow braced on the office counter. Ferd Mendoza sat in the shadows of the far corner in a straight chair with a blanket across his lap and his splinted leg protruding stiffly to rest on a stool. Across the room, Clabe Peabody reclined in the rocking chair with his shotgun on the floor.

Brack straightened. "Your name Kelly?"

Strangely, for all his aggressive bearing, Brack's voice was almost mournful. Kelly curiously studied him and eased aside to take his outline off the light in the open doorway.

He believed he detected bafflement and suffering beneath that stormy front and asked quietly: "Why did you have to mix in it, Brack?"

"They're my boys."

"Strawn, too?"

McQuail grimaced. "You can have Strawn."

"I have to have all three."

McQuail pride and harshness boiled up to consume the hurt. "You ain't gonna get 'em."

"Brack—how much do you know?"

"It don't make any difference."

Kelly spoke aside: "Mr. Peabody, Feeney would like for you to come out in the side yard with him." He waited until Peabody took up his shotgun and crossed the room in a shuffling yaw with his attention dragged back in suspicion to McQuail.

Kelly said, "So you're going to back your outfit to break in here after this Mexican family?"

"The Mexicans don't interest me!" McQuail retorted.

Kelly faced him across the silent room and thought Brack's admission was clear.

"McQuail, how long have you known?"

172

Brack bored his unblinking gaze into Kelly. "Since while ago when I talked to 'em at the wagonyard. They defied me, first time in their lives. That goddam Strawn's got some kind of a hold on my boys. They argued they had to finish a job on account of Blackie Toyah, but I know it wasn't that. I can read a man. Then Strawn butted in to say I'd better let my men take care of the Mexicans and Kelly, too, if I didn't want bigger trouble. He gave something away. I don't know what. I don't know if I want to know."

"You don't know what trouble he referred to?"

"I found out once that Strawn was a hired gunman up in Kansas. I know my boys acted hangdog that time they brought him back and brought my cattle money. It's been gnawin' me a long time. Then you show up. People may have different opinions about Brack McQuail, but nobody ever took me for a fool. Nobody but my own sons, looks like. There's some bad blood back somewhere between you and my boys and Strawn. I haven't put my finger on it, but I don't like the way it smells. I'm afraid what it may be like and it makes me sick clear to the bottom of my guts. But you ain't goin' to hurt them or me, Kelly. Whatever it is. Because I just ain't goin' to stand for it."

Kelly said softly, "You have a right to be sick, Brack. You raised them."

"None of your goddam put-in! I'm not here to be lectured on my failin's or make pussyfoot palaver. I just want to know, what do you aim to do?"

"Do you know Shep's a suspect in the murder of Jeb Mott?" He tossed that out, for a test, and was not surprised when it got nowhere.

"He denies it!" Brack snapped. "He's convinced me and that's all that's necessary. No damned upstart deputy sheriff is goin' to arrest him for that."

"No, he didn't kill Mott. It's not that, McQuail."

"Then it's this other thing. Whatever it is."

Feeney's head showed briefly at a side window. "Kelly, the bunch is comin' out of the saloon."

"All right. Keep watching and let me know—McQuail, if I told you what it is, the exact truth about your boys and Strawn, would it make any difference?"

McQuail hesitated. For an anxious moment, Kelly held to the hope that he might make an ally out of McQuail. Then the true McQuail arrogance came out, and the hope faded.

"It wouldn't make a damn bit of difference! No goddam scar-faced deputy sheriff I never saw before is coming in here and try to make a big name for himself by taking my boys off to jail. You can give up that smart-alec idea right now and you can get to hell out of town. I'll take care of the rest of it my own way."

"It's not just a country deputy that's after them, Mc-Quail."

"I don't care if it's the whole county."

"More than the county."

"Then who?"

Kelly said flatly: "The United States."

McQuail jerked. His thicket of gray brows ran together in a massive frown. "What does that mean?"

"I'm a Deputy U.S. Marshal. The crime is a federal one. Does that make it any different?"

Brack looked haggard. He bent and peered closely at the badge Kelly wore. His vision glazed over cold, then turned hot again as he recovered and stubbornly shook his head. "Not a damn bit. You can have Strawn. My boys are my blood and I'll stand up for my own."

Kelly heard Ferd Mendoza's short cough. From somewhere outside Feeney called urgently, "They're comin' this way, Kelly! The whole bunch—"

Kelly half turned to the window to reply to Feeney and heard Mendoza cough again. The corner of his eye caught the hall entrance and he knew that Maria and Alice had been standing there. In the second that his attention was diverted he heard Brack's movement, the slide of steel against leather, and a low exclamation from Alice. He whirled back.

174

The big blue gun was raised in Brack's steady hand.

"You lift 'em, Kelly."

He saw Brack's finger tighten on the trigger. He raised his hands.

"Walk ahead of me out the back," McQuail ordered. "You're ridin' out of the country."

"And if I don't?"

"Then I'll kill you on the spot and let that crowd tear this place apart, Mexicans and all." His stare burned in crazed purpose that left no doubt.

The flat *smack* of a muffled explosion broke the silence, and Brack stretched high on his toes, dropped his gun, and spun to clutch at the counter. He grabbed with one hand where the blood gushed at the base of his neck. Kelly's gun whipped into his hand, covering Brack, whose muscles began to give way. He sagged to his knees, then fell heavily to his side on the floor.

Kelly called, "Maria—quick! Stop the blood with something!"

He glanced at the far-corner shadows. Ferd Mendoza's right hand was still under his blanket laprobe. Ferd worked his left fingers to pinch out smouldering fire where smoke curled through a hole in the fabric. He threw the blanket aside and the revolver was there with smoke drifting from its snout.

Mendoza pushed himself up from the chair and hobbled across to look down at Brack McQuail. Kelly made a gesture of commendation and said, "You pulled me out of a bad fix."

"Saw what he was working up to and tried to warn you. I only meant to wing him. Maria, see what you can do for the man."

Maria sat on the floor and took Brack's head into her lap. Alice brought a cloth which Maria wadded and pressed firmly against the flow of blood. "Someone should get the doctor."

Kelly hurried out to the porch. The first buildings south

and the trees at the road bend cut off direct view of the business street. He called, and Feeney jogged from the trees, across the open space.

"What happened in there?"

"McQuail's shot. He could die if we don't get Doc Rice here."

"A fine time!" Feeney grunted. "Somebody would have to walk through that mob to find him."

Kelly heard the light footsteps behind him. Alice came onto the porch. "I'll go, Saul. We can't just let the man bleed to death."

"You can't go out there!"

She stopped, her body stiffening in dread. They all heard the approaching sounds of men beyond the road bend. Then a high-pitched yell cracked the air. Behind the trees a gunshot sounded and the slug splashed adobe on the high edge of the station's south wall.

13.

Feeney nervously bobbled his rifle. But there was nothing yet to aim it at; just sounds beyond the bend, high sun glinting on the tops of the intervening trees. "Some drunk," Feeney muttered. "He'll try for a window next."

A thunderous *boom* sounded from the back of the station and Kelly and Feeney both jumped. The shotgun had answered the rifle spat.

"An old trigger finger got itchy," Kelly muttered. He stepped to the end of the porch and yelled, "Peabody!" The old man eased around the back corner, bent over as if stalking game. He approached in a crouch against the side of the building.

"What was that shot for, Peabody?"

"Why, they plinked one at us. I just gave 'em one back over the trees." He winked before guiltily hanging his head.

"You go inside. Put that shotgun on the floor and don't pick it up again until I say so."

Peabody obediently trudged to the entrance and disappeared.

The sounds approaching on the road needed no identification but Feeney said uneasily, "Here they come," and Kelly murmured, "I can hear." His blood rang with it; he could hear nothing else.

"Not much of a stand two can make, Kelly."

"You afraid, Feeney?"

177

"Might as well admit it. Ain't you?"

"I guess I am." Kelly attempted to smile. Feeney did not look afraid; just resigned to short odds and seeing no way out.

Kelly said, "What I've been afraid of is that they would never come to me."

He glanced back and saw that Alice still lingered at the doorway. Her gaze held on him, wide with fear. "Please go inside, Alice. Lock the door."

"I am afraid for you, Saul."

"Hurry. Get inside."

"Saul—it is no good. Don't try to fight them. They are too many."

That was the truth and he knew it. Coming beyond the road bend was big trouble, a primed powder keg, and violence rampant if the issue got out of hand. *Damn it, Wendel, couldn't you organize any help?* He supposed that all Grande Flat was now barricaded within their homes.

He slid his Colt up and down in its holster. His hand felt too slick. He tried to dry the sweat with swipes across his shirt.

Feeney said petulantly, "What in God's name do they want, actually?"

"By now that bunch doesn't truthfully know what they want. Whisky and big talk have just ignited something. Maybe their personal offense at Mexicans defying orders."

According to the sounds, the advancing crowd had slowed. He supposed that Bert would be giving instructions, the general firing up his troops.

"Know what I look for, Kelly?"

"What?"

"They'll try to burn us out."

"Yes. That would be the easy way. One can of coal oil and one match in the barn would settle the whole issue."

"Mighty right. All Miz Mendoza would own then would be a big pile of ashes."

Kelly glanced back to make sure that Alice had gone in-

178

side. The door was closed. "Feeney, you watch for one of them carrying a coal oil can and use that rifle. Aim for his leg."

Maria spoke at the side window to Kelly's right. "Señor McQuail is unconscious, Saul. He has lost much blood."

"Well, stop the bleeding the best you can. There's just no way to get Doc Rice here now."

A glimmer of hope worked in his mind. A way to detract Bert, perhaps to turn back the mob, or at least gain a reprieve. He worked his Colt again, trying its slide within the leather, and dried his hand once more.

"Feeney, no matter what happens, I want Strawn."

"Why him, 'specially?"

"He's the man prodding the McQuails. Also the man I've been looking for ever since one night in the Territory.

Feeney shrugged. "You'll have to be damned fast to get him, according to what I've heard."

"I am damned fast," said Kelly quietly. "Ever since a man named Dick Hubbard was murdered, I've made it my prime job to be fast when the time came. And I think it's here."

Ferd Mendoza spoke from the window. "Saul? We don't like this. Nothing is worth it if you get killed. We'd rather run."

He could see Alice's tear-streaked face dimly back of Ferd.

"Sounds like Alice said that."

"Well, I say it, too."

"Now none of that kind of talk, Ferd. Pull the window shade and keep everybody on the far side of the room."

The sound of many trudging feet came again. Kelly and Feeney stood still in the shadows, watching from the end of the porch. The marchers began to emerge into view at the sandy bend in the stage road. There were about twenty but to Kelly they seemed to keep pouring out like a straggle of giant ants, some of them brandishing their rifles and hand guns. He recognized Bert's towering figure striding ahead.

The men slowed where the coach road forked into the station yard. Bert came a few steps ahead.

"Kelly! We'll give you two minutes to bring those Mexicans out here. You do that and nobody will get hurt."

Kelly stepped from the porch edge into the yard. He watched Strawn, and at the same time sought to locate Shep.

He noticed that Strawn was drifting aside from the halted cluster. On the opposite flank, he saw Shep angle toward the backyard, and he knew that this was Bert's plan. He could not watch Strawn and Shep at the same time.

"Feeney, you there behind me?"

"I'm here, Kelly."

"The man moving in the side yard—keep your rifle on him." Feeney advanced to the corner with his rifle half raised. Kelly called, "Shep! Stop right there." Shep halted.

Kelly watched Strawn from the corner of his eyes as he called out: "Bert! Listen to me—Brack's in here, bad wounded. He needs Doc Rice, quick. You hear me, Bert?"

Strawn warned, "It's a damned trick—"

Bert roared, "You're lyin'! Pa went home—"

"Then send a man in here to look!"

Shep's position had given him an open view to the back. He called incredulously: "Bert! The old man's horse is yonder at the pen gate!"

Kelly saw uncertainty seize Bert, and his ponderous effort to think. Bert turned a haggard, questioning glance across to Strawn as if asking for a moment of clemency.

Strawn shook his head. His gun hand hung straight down. He wiggled his fingers. Kelly knew, then, that the two McQuails were hopelessly trapped. Strawn, the shrewd professional, had hooks forever set into the two blundering McQuail sons, the victims of their own past and now the victims of their Arbuckle Canyon henchman.

The men in the scattered stand behind Bert showed that they had caught the hesitation in their leader. Their talk died. They shuffled uneasily. Kelly tried again: "Your pa's dying, Bert—"

"It's a trap!" Strawn repeated. "Move on up, men—we want those Mexicans—"

The range was still extreme, for a hand gun. Strawn would want to close the distance. Kelly, watching him, said, "You men back there—it will pay you to listen to me instead of Strawn. This is not just a Mexican chase. I'm here as a Deputy U.S. Marshall to arrest Bert and Shep and Strawn for robbery and murder. Now let that soak in. It's their private trouble, and now's the time for you to pull out of it."

The delegation stayed immobile with their grim faces set on him, as if the minds behind them labored to sort his words and to find their own roles in a jumble not clearly understood. Bert appeared to sag. He licked his lips.

Kelly said, "Bert, your pa could die if you don't get Doc Rice—"

Bert dragged another pleading look to Strawn. Strawn said shortly, "Don't let him take you in with that lie—"

Kelly snapped, "You look at the window, Bert—" He raised his voice. "Peabody! Maria! You hear me? I want Brack McQuail shown at the window. Pull him over and hold him up—"

Peabody yelled from inside, "Just a minute—" and Kelly heard the heavy weight slide slowly toward the window.

The strained attention of the men in the road shifted to the window.

First the windowshade rattled, shooting to the top, and Peabody's white-bearded outline showed briefly, and his shotgun, as the old man made a precautionary look outside. He bent out of sight, and Kelly could hear the mumble of directions. There were sounds of straining and lifting, and a long low moan. Then the upper part of Brack McQuail's body appeared to float upward into view at the window like a body rising from a dark pit. Brack's chin hung to his chest and his head dangled limply sideways. Peabody and

181

the stout Nita could be seen straining to hold him there, with their hands clutched under his armpits and back, and Maria was barely visible where she reached her arm to continue to press a blood-soaked wad of cloth to the wound low in Brack's neck.

The limp apparition faded downward into the shadows in an eerie disappearance as hands lowered Brack's dead weight to the floor.

The bunched men stayed unmoving.

A shudder seized Bert from his thick neck to his boots. He found his voice and thundered: "Who killed him, Kelly?"

"Why, you may have killed him yourself, Bert. *That night in Arbuckle Canyon.* Maybe you would like to know—the one that you *did* kill—he was just the son of the Governor of Texas."

The shocked silence held. Kelly wiggled off the stiffening tension in his gun hand, seeing Strawn plainly without directly looking at him. The prod had switched to Strawn now. The hard stares of the group had turned on him. Their Mexican chase, starting as a kind of boozed-up celebration, had turned into something else. An invisible change somehow left Strawn standing apart, in something more than just distance. It was what Kelly had hoped for: the chance for the final play between himself and Strawn alone. His hand felt dry, his position felt right. He was ready whenever Strawn was.

Then Shep McQuail suddenly went to pieces, diverting both Kelly and Strawn. The shock of what he had seen at the window started Shep trembling. In a wild half-sob he screamed, "You made 'em kill Pa, Strawn! Oh you goddam dirty bastard—you forced it—" and he insanely began an unsteady walk toward Strawn across the open space.

Bert just stared, paralyzed. Shep was too clumsy in hand and brain, and all the watching eyes could see it. He drew his gun in fumbling slowness. Strawn drew and fired in practiced, professional speed. His second shot followed

182

quicker than the bat of an eye, smashing into Shep already dead. Shep fell buckled in the weeds with his gun and his hat beyond one outstretched arm and never moved again.

Imploringly and needlessly, Bert called brokenly, "Shep! Shep!—"

Strawn jogged a few steps forward, closing the distance to Kelly and with his gun still in his hand. The giveaway was when he had to stop, planting his right foot forward to brake himself.

Kelly made his draw.

Strawn's first shot fanned past his head, splashing the adobe dust. Kelly felt his gun bounce in his hands as he triggered with the draw, all one continuous act, and Strawn already was falling when he fired at Kelly the second time. But his gun sagged in his hand. Strawn's mouth worked in soundless talk as he staggered and Kelly fired again.

Bert stared at Strawn stretched dead in the dirt.

Kelly called thickly, "Your turn, Bert."

Bert kept his hand well out from his gun butt. Imploringly, he looked back to the men unmoving behind him. He screamed, "Kill 'im, men—" but not a gun was raised.

Feeney, who had been crouched just back of Kelly, side-stepped and brought his rifle up. "You fellers just look yonder—"

Heads turned.

Then Kelly saw them, too—the thin line of the town men rounding the road turn, a dozen or more with rifles and shotguns and the gaunt figure of Wendel leading them.

There was Doc Rice, with a shotgun raised, and Jonesy, and Si Minnow, and even Joe the barkeep, and a collection of others not known to Kelly.

He called softly: "Well, Bert? You want to draw?"

Bert turned back, rigid. Numbly, he shook his head.

"Don't kill me, Kelly. I want to give up."

"Pull your gun with your left hand. Slow. Now drop it— Walk over here, Bert."

The high fluffy suds of thunderheads momentarily

dimmed the early afternoon sunlight. The prairie breeze fanned the aisle of broomweeds as Bert plodded through, and the overhead haze draped a peculiarly subdued tone of gray dusk on the course of his lonely walk. The men kept immobile and silent. The scene was as if lights had been turned low, into an artificial twilight, to end a sorry day. Each set of eyes in the yard followed Bert's abject journey to his surrender.

"Bring the handcuffs from the office drawer," Kelly told Feeney.

Bert paused only once on his course, when he passed Shep's body. His stride dragged for a few steps. He turned his head away from his brother, and came on.

When Bert's wrists were locked behind his back, Kelly gestured for Doc Rice. "Get in there and do everything you can to save Brack."

Wendel had halted his force in an uneven battle line to the right of the McQuail crowd. Now the thunderheads sailed high on their way, uncovering the sun, and its light struck again over the prairie. Both sets of uneasy men were etched again in the harsh outlines of their mutual apprehension. They traded uncomfortable looks. Kelly suggested, "You want to say something, Wendel?"

Wendel faced the McQuail group and spoke tiredly. "You men got railroaded into something that was uglier than it looked. Now's the time we all put our guns away. There's been death enough in Grande Flat." He paused to dourly look them over. "I just have this to say: Anybody that wants to make more trouble, you've got us to contend with. Not only now, but from here on. This stage station property has passed into the ownership of the Mendoza family. They aim to stay right here and run it. We aim to see that they get a peaceable chance to do it. Anybody got any objections, let's hear you speak up now."

One of the posse replied quietly: "We don't want any trouble with Grande Flat, Mr. Wendel."

A piercing yell somewhere south broke the silence. Kelly

184

remembered; and now he could hear the pound of running hoofs and the rattle of wheels. The Thursday stage was making its usual grandiose entrance into town. Closer now, the driver let out his high whoop, his way to have his glory moment as he whipped up for a final spurt through main street to liven the sleepy town.

The two armed groups backed farther apart to clear the entrance road. The stage came on, slowed, and made the turn. The mustangs plunged and fought, frightened by the strange reception. The driver strained on the lines. The shotgun guard beside him craned his neck in startled looks to one side and the other.

A hand grasped Kelly's arm and he knew Alice had come to stand beside him.

Feeney had directed Bert to stand a few paces down the side wall. Peabody stood erect with his shotgun at port. The driver demanded, "Can't somebody take ahold of them bridles?" Two men from the McQuail group instinctively came forward to quiet the team. The guard swung down from the high seat. The driver met him at the coach door and reached to open it, and both of them, at the same time, stared at the bodies in the yard.

The town men on their side of the ruts gave space and began to touch their hat brims as Clarice Mott, dressed in black, and Connie Wendel hurried in from the clay sidewalk.

Connie's glance recoiled from the bodies of Strawn and Shep, swept to find Kelly with Alice beside him, and lowered again without recognition.

The first passenger to alight was Mrs. Otto Wendel, composed and impressive in her dark satin travel suit and small plumed hat. Four other passengers emerged after her and stayed huddled close together with strained and inquiring expressions.

Watching Mrs. Wendel, Kelly noticed there was something almost regal in her bearing as she slightly drew her skirt and walked to meet her approaching daughters. Clarice ran the last few steps, calling "Mother!" and Mrs. Wendel

185

embraced her as the new widow pressed her face to her mother's bosom. Wendel came to stand beside Connie, looking out of place in his black suit, string tie, and Winchester rifle dangling in his long arm.

When he had the chance, Wendel spoke in an undertone into his wife's ear. Kelly followed her quick glance toward the porch where Maria Mendoza had come to the doorway. With all eyes on her, Mrs. Wendel walked over, smiled, and like a returning friend, extended her hand to Maria. They exchanged murmured words, then Mrs. Wendel smiled again and walked back in easy dignity to join her husband and daughters. Kelly's glance caught Wendel's briefly and he nodded his appreciation.

The exit of the Wendel family to the street seemed to allow the halted spectators to move again. The driver stridently demanded, "What in holy hell's goin' on here?"

Thursday night closed down quietly upon a quiet town, silenced more than usual because Wendel had engaged a man to hammer up a temporary barricade across the broken doors of the darkened Texas Bar. He also had ordered a black veil wreath of mourning hung on the plank barricade in respect to the memory of the deceased owner.

The station was crowded, and the transients were bedded on cots. Brack McQuail occupied the former John Hinga bedroom, conscious again under the care of Doc Rice, assisted by Maria. Feeney and the coach guard spelled each other through the night, keeping watch over Bert handcuffed in the shed room. Kelly, the stage driver and Peabody spread blanket rolls in the hay loft of the barn.

Kelly slept the night through. He was at work early Friday, helping to feed and make the change in the six-mustang stage team, and getting it and its passengers on their way again. Later, he made a final visit with Wendal and also paid a courtesy call to Clarice before the funeral time. While Jeb's final rites were being conducted by Brother Tatum in the crowded church, Kelly assisted Feeney and a town man hired as guard, to start their ride with Bert on the journey south to the Kiowa City jail. Later, from there, he was to be transported to Austin for trial.

As the two men and their prisoner were about to depart, Bert asked morosely, "What will they likely do with me, Kelly?"

"Life sentence, if you're lucky."

Bert slumped low in his saddle. "Pa's goin' to live, ain't he?"

"Doc Rice says he is."

"Much obliged for letting me see him before I left."

"You're welcome, Bert."

Feeney said crisply, "Let's ride, boys." Their three horses filed out of the yard and were gone from town before the Mott mourners left the church.

Friday was the day for the southbound stage, more work to do, and another night of crowded sleeping quarters. In the two days, Kelly had not seen Alice alone. She had stayed busy helping with station details, assisting her mother to care for Brack, and helping Nita with the increased kitchen chores.

By mid-morning Saturday, Kelly was ready to leave. He had arranged for Peabody to remain with the Mendozas as a helper around the station, and it was also settled that Feeney would be given the job of running the freight wagons for Mendoza. Everything was attended to, he thought; or as well as he could do it. One thing unfinished, infinitely elusive, kept dodging from corner to corner of his mind and he was almost to the moment of departing before the answer burst as clear as a sunrise.

He was in the pen, his saddle roll packed and at the gate, his saddle and rifle boot ready, and was shaking out a noose to toss over his horse. He stalked the horse to a corner of the pen, threw the lariat, and the noose settled perfectly over the animal's neck.

The sound of handclapping startled him. He looked around and up.

187

Alice sat on the fence, applauding.

Kelly grinned self-consciously. She was performing the role of their younger years, and the memory flooded back to him—how Alice perched on the rail to watch him practice roping or breaking a colt.

He dropped the rope and pushed his hat back. She pressed her knees together and brushed down her skirt.

"Get down from there!"

"Why?"

"Ladies don't sit on top rails of horse pens."

"This lady sits where she chooses, to see the pen boy do his mighty stunts."

Kelly wiped his sleeve across his face and the blindness out of his mind forever. The composed brown features above him were set in an aloof expression. Her eyes squinted in penetrating study of him. The rise and fall of her breathing had stopped.

"Alice Mendoza, get down."

"Why, Saul Kelly?"

"Don't ask. Just come here."

Dutifully, she climbed down into the pen.

"Alice—I want—." He stopped. "Go pack your clothes."

"I have no other clothes. The fire—"

"Just that dress?"

"This is all. It covers me. Why?"

"I want you to go with me."

She cocked her head in doubtful analysis of him. All the sun in the sky collected in her eyes to make a glistening where the sudden mist formed.

"Where?"

He motioned to places far off. "Out there."

"To where you have been?"

"To everywhere I'll ever go."

"How you mean, I come with you?"

"Well, slightly illicit, I guess, for the first week of travel. Then we could be married in the Governor's mansion in

188

Austin. Dickie Hubbard would have been pleased. Governor Hubbard would expect that."

She struck a forefinger along her cheek and pretended to ponder. The pose did not dispel the sun and the mist.

"The Governor's mansion? Very well. I suppose that will be good enough."

He reached for her and she rushed into his arms, clinging tightly and whispering his name.

"Do you want to tell them goodby, while I try to hitch my horse to a buggy?"

"I'll just be a minute. They're all collected inside the kitchen door, waiting to see—"

He stared open-mouthed. "Waiting to *see?*" She laughed lightly and flew up and over the top rail in a flurry of brown bare legs.

He swung his bedroll and saddle and rifle into the back of a buggy, and hitched his horse, which bucked and fought the harness at first, until Kelly got him calmed to his new trappings of captivity.

Alice met him outside the gate and he helped her to the seat. In her one dress, with her hair blowing in fine black wisps from beneath her thin head scarf, she settled and waved to Ferd and Maria, Clabe Peabody and Nita, Jimmie and Doc Rice, all clustered on the back porch. Maria dabbed her apron edge to her eyes and Ferd saluted with his improvised hoe-handle crutch.

After that there was no time for further farewells. Once in the open side yard, the saddle horse acted up again, still hurt by the disgrace of harness and buggy, and tried to gallop. The buggy careened into main street. Alice clutched and bounced against Kelly and Kelly battled the reins. The City Mercantile flashed past, then Curley's Cafe, and the boarded-up Texas Bar and Minnow's wagonyard, and finally the shade-drawn Mott and Wendel houses, each dissolving behind them in rolling red dust. The buggy streaked south on the street, tore past the last dwelling and into the bend that would lose it in the upland spread of greasewood.

The last to see them was Mrs. Henrietta Forbes. The thunder of their passing jolted her erect from digging in her front-yard zinnia bed. She gazed after the dust and rattle until these vanished on the turn into the world beyond. She thought she had caught a fleeting glimpse of a small girl clinging with both arms around the neck of a man driving a runaway horse with only his left hand working the reins.

Will C. Brown is the pen name under which Clarence Scott Boyles, Jr., has written most of his Western fiction. Born in Baird, Texas, and descended from Texas cattle-raising families on both sides, Boyles's early career was in newspaper journalism. Although he did publish a couple of Western stories in pulp magazines in the 1930s, it was first following his discharge from the U.S. Marine Corps after the Second World War that he began his writing career in earnest. Texas is the principal setting in nearly all of Boyles's Western stories, including his first novel, *The Border Jumpers* (1955), which also served as the basis for the memorable motion picture, *Man of the West* (1958) starring Gary Cooper. Dell Publishing, which reprinted this novel, selected it to receive the Dell Book Award as the best Western novel of 1955. *The Nameless Breed* (1960) won the Golden Spur Award from the Western Writers of America in the category of best Western novel and is still considered to be Will C. Brown's *magnum opus*. A trek through the mile-wide *Valle de Cuchillos*, or Valley of the Knives, is the highlight of this story, vividly and harrowingly told. In these novels, as well as in *Laredo Road* (1959), *Caprock Rebel* (1962), and *The Kelly Man* (1964), a high level of suspense is established early and maintained throughout, often by characters being pitted against adverse elements and terrain. Boyles is particularly adept at making his readers feel the heat, dust, wind, desolation, deprivation, and dangers of the land in his stories. When violence does occur, it is logical and handled with restraint and brevity.